The Old Tramp's Coat

The Old Tramp's Coat

John Renshaw

First paperback edition 2023

ISBNs

Paperback: 978-1-80541-498-8
eBook: 978-1-80541-002-7

This book is dedicated to the only flower
I have ever truly appreciated, from
a very grateful old man.

1

Tom was plodding his way home. It had been a long harsh winter and a very wet spring. He had just finished planting the last of the seeds in his small field. He was aware that his effort could well be a waste of time due to the heavy, cold soil, but planting any later would have been a complete waste of time. So, wet and bedraggled, he entered his humble home. His two children were huddled around a pitiful fire trying to coax it to burn. Wet kindling tends to emit lots of smoke and very little heat!

There was no hot food and no warm water, so Tom was extremely downcast; in the depths of despair. He had tried very hard to feed his family and had failed. Sarah, his wife, knew that something had to be done, and done quite quickly. She helped her husband to take off his wet clothes and dress himself in the few dry clothes he had left. She gave Tom the few remaining coins from her purse and insisted he go to the local inn. He refused point blank to take the money, saying, "That money is for food, not drink!" Sarah yelled at Tom, "Get to the inn! Give me and the children time to get the fire going and prepare some hot food. Go!" He was very tired, so he did not feel like arguing. He put his wet cap back on and left. Sarah smiled; she did not like rows; all she wished for was for Tom to be warm and relaxed.

The man of the house was very morose, thinking that both the weather and his wife were very much against him. As he walked to the inn, Tom realised it had stopped raining at last. He cheered up somewhat and began to plan what he was going to do over the next few days.

Tom entered the tavern and was greeted by Silas Mimms, the landlord. Silas Mimms was not known for his extravagance; never had anyone seen Silas give away a free tankard of beer. He had been landlord of this inn for more than 30 years and he knew everyone in the village and would often be overheard commenting, "To the young future clients… look after them."

Silas often offered minor duties in return for ale - "Clean the yard," (already spotless) "weed the garden and cut the grass". Mr Mimms was never surprised by much. Often, when he opened the door in the morning, he would find a brace of rabbits, or a bag of veg waiting there. He never questioned who had supplied this bounty; he simply accepted that they were a thank you, a token of respect.

When Tom entered the inn, Silas observed his cap, wet through, and his clothes which were shabby, but at least they were dry and appeared cared for. To Silas, it was as if he was looking at a character from a book! "Pint please, Silas," said Tom. As the landlord started to pull Tom's pint, he noted the coins he had placed on the bar. Tom was short of cash by some margin. Silas almost stopped pulling the ale, hesitated, then completed the operation. "Have I enough money to pay for the ale?" Tom enquired.

Silas checked the cash and then replied to Tom, "You are a very lucky man! Your payment is spot on. Furthermore, that was the last pint out of the barrel. Next barrel, price goes up!" Tom was not fooled; he knew Silas too well. Silas went down to the cellar pretending to change the barrels. Tom sipped slowly at his ale; he had to make it last.

His gaze wandered to the far end of the room. A wonderful fire was blazing away. Sitting near the fire was an old man, smoking his pipe and quaffing his beer. Hot as the fire was, he had kept his coat on. He beckoned Tom over and bade him sit by the fire. They sat together, silent for a while, Tom drying his cap on his knee, the old man quietly content to smoke his pipe. It was Tom who began the conversation; "Old one," Tom asked, "how can you wear a heavy coat like that whilst sitting very close to the fire?"

"Dennis is my name, lad, so please use it when you address me. Regarding the coat, it keeps me cool in the summer and warm in the winter. Tattered and torn as it is, I have had this coat for over forty years. It was old when it was given to me as a gift." Tom was stunned and wondered how old the coat actually was. Dennis beckoned to him. "Feel the quality, Tom. It once belonged to a great man indeed and I will wear this coat with pride for as long as I live. It was given to me by a very old lady; sit back and I will tell you all about it. However, before I tell the story, I will get the drinks in!"

Tom protested; "There is no way I'm going to let a poor old man pay for my beer, especially when I cannot return the favour." Dennis's face contorted in anger. He then said, "My clothes may be old and shabby, but that does not mean I cannot afford to pay for the ale." Tom was mortified. He had insulted Dennis without meaning to. He humbly apologised to Dennis.

The old man, somewhat mollified, went to the bar for the refills. Deeply troubled, Tom wondered how much further he could sink into depression. The weather and his family seemed to be against him and now, he had deeply offended the old man. He gazed at the bar. Silas had pulled the pints, his hand resting on the bar, fingers tapping with impatience. Dennis pulled two coins out of his pocket and placed them on the bar. Silas just shook his head as if to say that was not enough. Once more, Dennis felt into his coat pocket and placed two more coins on the bar. One glare from the landlord told Dennis he was still short. Once more, into the pocket Dennis went, found two more coins, and placed them on the bar. Silas nodded; beer paid for. In the meantime, Tom had observed what was happening at the bar. It appeared to him that Dennis was struggling to pay for the drinks. Tom was angry with himself. He had let a poor old tramp pay for his drink! The drinks were placed on the table and Tom thanked the old man.

"Back to my tale," said Dennis. "It all began when I was in the Army fighting abroad. An old soldier had befriended me and, one night, he told me a strange story. He began… 'There lives an old lady in a faraway place, a woman of charm, of beauty and grace'…" Dennis rambled on. Tom, on the verge of falling asleep, no doubt due to the warmth of the fire and the beer he had drunk, paid little attention to the fairy tale he was being told. He caught the last few sentences of Dennis's story "… yes, I repeat, there is so much more gold and diamonds lying in the road that you could not carry away any more than a small portion of the treasure."

Tom did not believe a single word of the outrageous tale, but, out of politeness and filled with sarcasm, he asked, "How much gold did you bring back?"

Dennis gave a wry smile and said, "By my appearance, you are thinking, one, my story is a load of rubbish, and two, if he brought back gold, why is he dressed in those old rags? I will tell you, Tom. I came back with all the treasure that I needed to last me the rest of my life!" Tom and Dennis talked quietly for a few moments then they heard, "Time, gentlemen, please," from Silas. Dennis rose first, then Tom said hesitantly, "Dennis, if you wish to spend the night at my abode, you are very welcome to share whatever we have".

The old man thanked Tom for his generous offer, but declined the invitation, saying quite enigmatically, "I have always slept under the stars, and when I feel hunger, there is food in the fields, hedgerows and trees, fresh in the fields, river and seas; what more do I need?" And so, they parted. Dennis left and bade goodbye to Silas and Tom.

Tom drained his tankard, placed it on the bar and walked towards the door. Then Silas called out, "Can you spare me a moment, please?" Tom was astounded - it was the first time he had ever heard Silas say please! Tom walked back to the bar wondering what Silas wanted. For the first time that night, Tom observed that Silas looked drawn and worn out, showing clear signs that old age had caught up.

"Tom," Silas said, "are you busy tomorrow?" Tom was careful in his reply, as it was obvious this man was in sore need of help.

"All of my crops are planted, so I've nothing that cannot wait. I am at a loose end for a couple of hours, so can I be of help?" Silas was hesitant in what he wanted to say, disliking the very idea of asking for help.

"I am getting rather low on kindling and logs for my fires, so if you could cut some up for me, I would be very grateful. I insist on paying for your work; I will not accept charity." Tom told Silas he would come the next morning, "Provided, of course, that I set the terms and conditions of payment!" Silas reluctantly agreed.

Next morning, Tom and his son Don strolled down to the inn. Don was just over 13 years of age, a strong young man, older than his years in many ways. Tom was very proud of his lad - they had worked together very well indeed for a few years now. As Tom opened the barn door, something struck him as odd. He quickly realised what it was - there were no sounds from within whatsoever. For many years, Silas had kept at least one cow and two pigs. Yet now, the barn was empty!

Don pointed out that there was not much wood in there to cut. So unlike Silas, Tom thought. "Right, Don, let's cut what is left of the wood." It took less than an hour, so Tom suggested, "This will not last long, Don. Come, we will go to the small wood that Mr Mimms owns". The Mimms family had owned this wood for generations. It was kept very private, and very few people were allowed in. Tom and his son set off through the wood and soon found a couple of trees that had fallen; ideal for firewood. The big problem was how to get the fallen trees from the wood to Silas's barn. It was beyond the capabilities of both Tom and Don to move it manually, so Tom suggested they should go and speak to Silas about it. The short walk from the wood to the old farmhouse, which had since been converted into the inn, did not take long. Silas was waiting by the back door as he had observed them going towards the wood. Silas felt a bit miffed; he should have been asked for permission.

Tom approached Silas and told him about the fallen trees. He asked Silas if he had any ideas that might resolve the issue. "For as long as my family have lived here, the wood was always dragged up by horsepower," he said.

"Where is your horse?" asked Tom.

Silas replied, "Looking after my horse, cow and pigs became too much for me". He gave a long sigh, then admitted, "They had to go".

"As I walked back from the wood," said Tom, "I could not help but notice that your two meadows really need cutting. That would make fine winter feed for many livestock."

"Tom, I have neither the means nor the need to cut the grass; I have no stock to feed any more!"

Tom pondered for a while then said, "I may have a solution, but it means you will have to trust me."

For quite a while, Silas held his tongue. Then finally, he said, "It is obvious, Tom, that I am in dire need of help. These past few months have really got me down. I have reached the point where I have to trust someone, so just go ahead with whatever deal you have in mind, and, when things are done and dusted, just let me know the cost."

Father and son made their way back home for a bite to eat. Whilst consuming his meal, Tom told Don of his plans. "We will go and see Jackson," said Tom. Jackson was a local farmer, a big man, but with a very genial nature. This did not imply that Jackson was a soft touch - far from it! As usual, he was going about the farmyard, mending, patching, banging various tools and implements. His three sons were out in the fields as usual, tending stock or planting crops. However, as Tom and Don ventured to enter the yard, a loud barking from the old dog stopped them in their tracks!

Jackson appeared out of one of the buildings, shooed the dog away and beckoned Tom and his son inside. Jackson spoke, as always, in a very broad local dialect. "Nah, Tom, young 'un, nowt to do in field, eh?" Tom outlined his plan to Jackson, and for a while no one spoke. "Ah tha telling me that tha wants to loan me Jenny" (Jenny was a giant of a horse, a Suffolk punch) "and in reton, she mows Silas' fields an ah keeps mown hey for meself?"

Tom replied, "Yes, Jackson".

Jackson scratched his grizzled jaw, and muttered indistinctly, "Ah tha tellin' me that Silas has got rid of his stock?" Tom told Jackson that he did not know why the innkeeper had let his stock go and added that Silas had kept a few hens and a couple of goats. In his own methodical way, Jackson pondered. At last, he said, "Two days' time, thee and young 'un be here at daybreak to take yon nag down t'wood. Tha can have 'oss for 2 hours only!" Tom was pleased with the deal. The old blown-down trees would be taken to the landlord's barn and over the coming weeks, he and Don would chop them up for Silas's winter fuel. He informed Silas of the deal he had done with Jackson. It pleased Silas, who said, "Thank you very much, Tom".

Two days later, at the crack of dawn as per the agreement, they entered the farmyard fully expecting to put chains, collars, tack, etc. onto the horse, but she was ready. It took about two hours to move the fallen trees into Silas's stockyard. Once they were finished, they began cleaning Jenny with water and rags. Silas appeared and said to Tom and Don, "Here you are - my curry combs that I used to use on my horse. Also, there is some polish for her leathers".

It had passed noon by the time the pair of them were satisfied with their work. Jenny was led back to the farmyard. Jackson appeared and gazed at the horse open-mouthed in wonder! Old Jenny had never looked this good! He turned to Tom and Don. "Get out of my yard now! You pair have shamed me. Go!" Don was distraught as they walked home.

Neither of them could imagine what had caused Jackson to fly off the handle. Having consumed their lunch, they set off for the fields; after all, the weeding must be done.

When it came time for their evening meal, still feeling heavy-hearted, the two of them trudged their way home. Tom entered first and was amazed to see Jackson sitting at the table. He was sitting there, twisting his cap in his huge hands. It was more than obvious that he was a bag of nerves. Tom's gaze dropped to the table, which was loaded with various items, such as bacon, pork and eggs. "How tha doin?" asked Jackson. "Wife say she was overburden with such stuff." It went very quiet for a few moments. The old farmer spoke again; "Wife told me, 'Seeing as tha is goin' round Tom's to apologise for thy stupid remarks, tha may as well take this wi thee; it's all surplus anyroad'." Jackson told them he was very sorry for his loutish behaviour and asked if they would please forgive him.

Tom spoke first. "We did not mean to offend you at all. It's a grand gesture of you and your good lady to give us this food. Your apology, although not needed, does you credit." The old farmer mumbled his thanks.

"The worst part of this day was when I walked Jenny to her stable, wife stood outside door and shouted, 'You old fool, we do not want a new horse yet; fetch Jenny back now!'"

Jackson bade them farewell. As he opened the door, he hesitated and turned to Tom, who noticed a twinkle in his eye. "Nah then, Tom, ahm looking for someone to prepare old nag for the county show. It's in a few weeks' time. Not my idea, tha understands; the wife's. Ah told her it wer a waste of time, but she put her foot dern. Ah knows that thee and young 'un are busy doing thy own work, plus helping Silas, so I will none impose on thy good nature. So do me a favour and look for a young 'un to help me get old nag ready for show. I'd like answer in next two days." Jackson closed the door and as he strolled the half-mile home, he pondered on the day's events. He had verbally lashed out at Tom and Don; he was immediately contrite but they had left by then (in disgust at me, thought Jackson). His wife had laced into him. To his wife's surprise, Jackson agreed totally with her scolding. The upshot was to mollify her and enter Jenny in the county show!

Their daughter, young Sarah, gave Tom a glare, stamped her foot in temper at not being considered for the job and left the room. His wife just glared at him as she left to prepare the next meal. "Don," said his father, "you have to learn to understand people. Jackson and his wife have already made their choice; it's you! The old farmer does not like to ask for favours directly."

Then Don spoke; "But Dad, you have given Jackson your word that you will search the village for the next two days to find a suitable person to help him".

"I will never break my word," replied his dad. "Once given, my word is my bond, so I will look around the village as promised." Don was crestfallen.

"After you have found someone, will you tell me first, please?"

"I will," said Tom. "Two days from now, you will be the first to know, and Jackson and his wife will be second. Does that satisfy you?"

Tom made his first foray during the early hours of the morning; dawn was at least an hour away yet. He strolled around the village, not surprised that he saw not a living soul. He had kept his word; he had searched that day. Pleased with his efforts, he made his way home. He stopped at the gateway to rest a while, leaning on his arms on the gate. There was a full moon still in the sky and it was a bit breezy and cold. As he rested, a barn owl was hovering waiting to catch his breakfast. Suddenly, the owl swooped. It had caught its morning meal! Tom stood there for quite a while observing bats returning to their abode in the old barn, and spying two foxes far off in the distant hedgerow. They had seen Tom long before he had spotted them. Tom was totally at peace with himself. He had enjoyed the night's activities and looked forward to the next night's work!

Two days later, as promised, Tom and Don visited Jackson to let him know that Don was more than ready to help him prepare Jenny for the show. Jackson, of course, was delighted. "Nah then, young 'un," he said to Don. "Hatha in need of owt special to get owd nag ready?"

"Not really," was the reply. "Mr Mimms has said I can have the loan of his cleaning tackle; in fact, he stated that I could keep it. Not having a horse, he said he didn't need horse's tackle!"

Home to dinner they strode, Don planning his work for the following week - working on the small homestead, helping Silas, but most of all, looking forward to spending time with Jenny.

2

Tom and Sarah found more and more time for themselves. His fields did not need much attention now since his daughter was becoming very independent; as was Don, of course.

"Tom, you have seemed so very far away these past few weeks. What is bothering you?" asked Sarah.

"Nothing really," replied Tom. "Everything is going fine. Dan and young Sarah are more than pulling their weight around the farm, so I feel I am needed less and less."

"You are thinking of old Dennis again," said Sarah, "and are wondering if there is any truth in his story."

"Not really," replied Tom. "It's all a load of nonsense anyway. Streets paved with gold and diamonds and other such jewels!" Sarah made her mind up; she was aware that if she did not push Tom into going on this wild escapade, he would only brood on it for a long time, wondering to himself, 'What if...'.

"You are going," insisted Sarah. "We can manage on our own for a few months." Tom dithered and finally agreed. He must make the journey for his own peace of mind.

Tom set off the next day on his long journey, with no idea of the destination or how long it would take, and little realising that it would be over a year before he saw his family again. He had a few words from Dennis engraved on his mind - "Head for the coast, find a ship that is going to Europe, make for the hills, then search, my friend!" Tom strode along at a good walking pace, but by noon, he began to feel tired and hungry. After a rest and with his hunger and thirst dealt with, he set off once more. By nightfall, he must have walked over 20 miles. 'I must find a place to rest for the night,' Tom thought. In the distance, he could see a dwelling. 'I will ask if there is any work to do, then maybe in return, they might give me food and somewhere to rest.'

This way of finding food and rest continued until finally, Tom reached the coast, but he was still to find a port. As he rested awhile, Tom pondered on the journey so far. The different ways that he had been greeted when he asked for food in exchange for labour truly amazed him. Three had slammed the door in his face, and one of them had even discharged a shotgun over his head with a warning, "I will fire the next barrel in 20 seconds... BEGONE!" Tom ran away as fast as he could. That night was spent under a hedgerow with his only food being berries and nuts.

However, he had fond memories of three places on his journey. On the second day, Tom had called at a farm and, as usual, offered his labour in exchange for food. The burly farmer obliged him; "Chop that wood, clean out the stables then come to the back door for your grub." After two hours' hard graft, the chores were done, and as instructed, Tom reported to the farmer. "Here is thy supper. Eat it in the stables and bed yourself down for the night in the hay loft." Tom looked at his supper - two slices of bread and just a small portion of cheese! He thanked the farmer for his offerings and went to the hayloft to consume his food, then he slept. At daybreak, Tom rose, had a wash in the horse trough, then with his ablutions finished and his face wiped on his shirt, he began his pilgrimage once more.

However, as he reached the farmyard gate, he halted. The farmer was calling him. 'Not more work!' Tom groaned inwardly. "Wife insists you go to the kitchen; she has needs of thee." Tom duly turned around and strode back to the farmhouse, where the lady of the house bade him enter.

"Sit down at table, lad, thy breakfast is almost ready." Tom gazed with awe at the plate that was laid before him. He had heard of the baronial breakfasts, but surely this outdid even them! Eggs, bacon, sausage, black pudding and much more… even four slices of fried bread! Slowly, Tom ate, and, as he did so, he recounted his journey so far, telling Jane, the farmer's wife, of his aspirations for his pilgrimage. At last, his magnificent breakfast consumed, he sat there drinking his third mug of tea. Jane told him why his plate was so full. "In all the long years we have lived on this farm, Jed has never turned anyone away that 'as asked for food. He always told them all food will be given only after it is earned! Most did very little, yet complained at what was offered them, and most stayed the night in the hayloft and expected to be fed the next morning, but the idlers received nothing. In the past forty years, only four were given a meal the next day, and only two of them, including yourself, received the full breakfast. The first one, whose name I cannot recall, was so very like yourself; completed his allotted tasks and thanked Jed for his meagre supper. This pleased Jed immensely, as did your work. Jed inspected your labours after you had retired for the night, then said, "Give that man a FULL meal in the morning; he deserves it, Jane!"

Tom said, "Was his name Dennis?"

Jane was stunned; "How did you know?"

"I have met him only once a few months ago. Dennis regaled me with a fairy tale about a faraway land. At first,

I imagined it was nothing more than an old man's rambling and yet I could not dismiss it from my brain. So, here I am on a foolish quest to God knows where, leaving my family to fend for themselves. I must appear to be a complete idiot!"

"A fool you may be, Tom, but live your dream because if you do not, you may regret it for the rest of your life!" Tom bade them goodbye and continued on his journey.

Fully revived now, Tom strode along. Courtesy of Jane, he also had a packed lunch to look forward to; bless her and Jed for their kindness. He would never forget them.

Nightfall came and Tom slept in an old abandoned house. Still having some of the packed lunch left, Tom was content with life.

The Wayside Inn stood just on the outskirts of a small village, and although it was only mid-afternoon, Tom needed a rest and some food. As he approached the inn, it was obvious to him that the outside surroundings had been somewhat neglected. "Maybe a chance of work here?" he wondered. He entered the inn and was greeted by a rather stout lady. "Yes, sir, what may I offer you to drink?" Tom admitted quite openly, "I have no money, however, in return for tidying up outside, or any other work you may have for me, all I ask for is food and shelter for the night". Susan, the licensee, gazed at him with a shrewd look on her face. "It is true that the yard is in dire need of attention; very well, lad, get cracking!"

'Still a few hours of daylight left,' thought Tom, 'enough time to complete the work.' It was almost dark when he completed his tasks. "Now for a meal and perhaps some rest in a nice warm bed," he murmured hopefully. The tap room was very busy, with the usual pub games being played - darts, dominoes, cards. Exchanges of banter flowed across the tables, and the air was heavy with tobacco smoke. Tom approached the bar then hesitated; he had no money to buy a pint. He turned around as if to go out again then a voice called him back. "Tom, come to the bar! What do you want to drink?" Tom asked for a pint of bitter and was very thankful to receive it. "When you have drunk that, come back for a refill," said Susan.

The local loudmouth was being served at the same time and noted that no money had been given to Susan. "Hey up, lads, free beer for Susan's fancy man, so play your cards right and all might get free ale!" Without touching his beer, Tom fled, bright red with embarrassment. The room rang with laughter. Susan leaned over the bar and grabbed the instigator of the mirth by the throat. "You, Jack Sharp, are banned for the rest of your life! I will not be serving any more beer tonight, and furthermore, this inn is now closed for a long time, so BEGONE, ALL OF YOU, NOW!"

After the last man had left, Susan locked up then searched for Tom, but it was a futile quest for by this time, Tom was at least two miles away, searching for somewhere to rest his weary head and empty stomach. The late summer night found him in a small meadow, cosy but hungry, his last stay before he reached the coast. He had wandered down a leafy lane knocking on various doors asking for work, always receiving the same response - "GO AWAY!" 'Only two more houses to call at,' he thought. He looked long and hard at this house; the gardens were pristine; in fact, they were immaculate. However, he was starving. 'Nothing ventured, nothing gained,' Tom thought. He made his way up the garden path and rapped on the door. An old lady answered, demanding, "What do you want?" She glared at Tom in a suspicious manner, then Tom explained his predicament.

"For a little food, I will do anything. I am not needed in the garden, that is obvious, however, I am a handy type of person. I can mend, paint, almost all tasks around the home." The old lady, Ena, was warming to Tom. 'Poor he may be,' Ena thought, 'but I do like his manners and openness.'

"You are offering to work yet I see no tools about your person; how can you work without tools?"

Tom replied with candour, explaining about his pilgrimage. "I will succeed or die in the attempt; please believe me on this."

"I will show you the work, Tom, and regarding tools, there are plenty in the sheds, so just help yourself to what you require. None have been used since my dear husband passed away many years ago. By now, some of them may be beyond redemption, but that is for you to discover!"

Tom entered the house. To say he was shocked was an understatement! The gardens were fabulous, whereas the inside looked worse than a council tip! 'Why?' he pondered. Then Ena explained; "For many years, I have suffered ill health, and, unable to clean much, my needs are provided for by the local tradesmen; everything is brought to the door. Ron, my gardener, is a wonderful person but he will not enter the house and when I asked him why, he replied, 'It is not proper or fitting for a lone man to enter the house of a lone woman'.

Many are the times I have bade him enter, explaining that during inclement weather I could find him work inside, but all to no avail."

'Where to start…' thought Tom. 'I can only do so much in the time that I have.' Then, an idea formed in his mind. "When is Ron due again?"

"Tomorrow," replied Ena.

"Just an idea forming in my mind, that's all, but are you sleeping on the couch, Ena?"

"Due to health problems and loose treads on the stairs, it has been many years since I have used my bed. It must look dreadful upstairs. I shudder to think about it."

"In that case, Ena, I will start in this room. The skirting boards are hanging loose, the doors need adjusting, and the carpets need cleaning, as do the windows."

Many hours later, Tom sat down to a meal. They chattered for a while about various matters. Ena told Tom of her late husband's life as a captain of many vessels on the high seas, and of his wise investments that had left her a wealthy widow. She had no living relatives whatsoever. Tom sat there digesting what she had told him and thought to himself, 'All that this old lady craves is company and someone to take care of her. What a sad state of affairs this is!' He vowed to himself to do something about it. "Ena, with your permission, I will stay for three more days to do what I can. Is that suitable to you?"

Ena jumped at the offer; "If only you could stay longer, that would be my dream, Tom!"

"Time for rest, Ena. See you in the morning." Tom climbed the stairs very carefully, testing each tread as he went. There were three loose treads but nothing broken - all that was needed was tapping in the small wedges that held the treads in place. 'That's the first job in the morning,' thought Tom.

Every bedroom was in a disgusting state, so he chose one then slept. As daylight hit the grimy window, Tom rose, his day already planned. Quietly, he made his way downstairs in case Ena was still asleep. To his surprise, breakfast was almost ready! "I too rise with the sun, Tom. Sit down, please, and eat!"

With the meal consumed, he told Ena some of his ideas. "The stairs I can mend, however, all the rooms above are beyond redemption. The curtains, bedding, most of the furniture and almost all of the clothes need dumping as all have been ravaged by moths, mildew and damp. I also believe the house needs a complete rewire, the heating system is in a poor state, and a re-plaster throughout is essential. I am sad for being the bearer of such news. I do have plans for ensuring the works are done, but no doubt it will be costly and take time. Are you happy with my proposals?"

"Money is no problem; my only concern is the noise, dust and disruption, especially as you are planning to leave soon. Regarding upstairs, please dump everything unless you find items that you can use or take with you."

"If my plans bear fruit, you will move away for a few weeks and, when you return, all will be pristine."

"Please go ahead and carry out your plans, Tom!" said Ena.

3

"GET OUT OF THERE, YOU THIEF!" Tom had been so busy sorting out tools that he had failed to hear Ron's approach. Tom spun round sharply at the sound of the voice. A raised spade was in Ron's hands, ready to strike Tom over the head should there be a need!

"Morning, Ron," said Tom as he offered his hand to shake.

Ron looked dumbfounded. "How do you know my name?"

"Ena has told me all about you, Ron. Please, come inside and take a seat whilst I explain matters. By the way, I do admire what you have achieved in the gardens - they look magnificent!" So, for the next few minutes, Tom brought him up to date with the situation and why he needed Ron's help in the house.

Ron said, "I feel ashamed of myself finding out that the old lady has been living in such circumstances. I could have helped so much. All this upset is down to me, because of my beliefs of what is the correct thing to do. How could I have been so stupid! Never again will I let this happen!"

"First of all, Ron, we need a lorry. Can you get one today?"

"Old Mick in the village has a small three-ton lorry; he may oblige us if he is not busy. Mick does odd-jobbing around the local area, so if I go now, I may catch him in. What do I offer him?"

"His usual rates, plus 50% bonus if he is here before midday. Also, it would be great if you could please bring your family back with you to keep Ena company."

Ron was back within the hour accompanied by his wife and two children. "Mick is coming; your terms are agreeable but he wants cash - no cheques!"

They began emptying the upper rooms and storing the waste on the drive. Ena was busy playing with the children, teaching them how to paint, sketch, and do puzzles. Ena was loving every moment of it all! Ron's wife, Madge, had already lit the boiler and soon filled it with Ena's bedding. Despite Ena's protests of having no clean bedding, Madge said, "That does not matter one jot. I will not have you living in these conditions, so until the work is completed to my satisfaction, you will stay with us!" Ena was too stunned to argue - just a nod of her head and a thank you.

Mick arrived at noon and the first load was duly dispatched to the local tip. By the end of the day, he had completed four journeys to the tip. All the upper floor was now bare. The only things saved were a few pictures, four gold coins, a fair amount of silver and many letters, plus a pair of seaman's boots and a duffel coat for himself. Mick was happy with his pay. Meanwhile, Ena had left with Ron and Madge.

Tom was alone and very content; a small meal then bed. Ron turned up bright and early ready to get rid of the clutter from the ground floor. Mick came about midday and the lorry was soon loaded. Maybe two more journeys to the tip would suffice for the time being. Noon came and it was time to rest and enjoy a packed lunch. As they ate, further plans were discussed. To Tom's delight, Ron had turned out to be a knowledgeable person indeed, and Tom was content that he could leave Ron to engage and manage tradespersons as and when required. One thing puzzled Tom, "The old lady, Ron, always has money about her and yet she can barely walk down the drive. How and where does she get the cash?"

Ron smiled. "Every so often, Ena hands me an envelope and in it there is a note signed by Ena. This I take to the bank then I am handed back a sealed envelope with cash inside which I hand back to Ena on my return." Fully satisfied with all aspects of the money matters, Tom was happy that the workmen could be paid, the project was in good hands and soon he could continue his quest. Two more days passed by and at last, the gutting of the house was finished - every ceiling, door, skirtings and all the old plaster had been removed and the final load of debris gone. The removal of the window frames was to be left to the joiner. The copper was filled with water and the fire lit. Soon, the water was warm enough for a bath. A tin bath had been found outside; now, it would be put to its final use!

Tom had just recommenced his pilgrim's journey, all rigged out in the deceased captain's clothes, when he heard a shout. "Where are you going?" It was Ron.

"To complete my journey," answered Tom.

"No, you are not, not until you have visited Ena!" Tom was surprised and pleased to hear Ron speak with such authority. He was now certain the house was in good hands. As they strolled along, Ron gave Tom a programme of works for Ena's house.

"Commencing next Monday, the electrician will begin the first fix along with the joiner, who will take up floorboards as required by various trades and first-fix joinery will progress as and when. The bricklayer will start during that week and his first job is to remove the old fireplaces, plus do necessary work for the installation of central heating and new surrounds. The second week sees the commencement of plastering works, followed by the plumber's initial work, and all other trades will attend as and when. All in all, I estimate completion and ready for occupation will be in about three months." Tom was very impressed with Ron's meticulous planning.

As they neared Ron's house, Tom became aware of the poor state of the property. Two leaning chimneys and cracked walls were obvious. 'Why?' thought Tom.

His companion noticed Tom looking at this tumbledown abode then said, "Many times, I have asked the landlord to do repairs, always getting the stock reply, "It will be done in time!" Inside the home, the place was clean and comfortable despite the many cracked walls and missing plaster.

"Be seated, Tom," said Ena, "whilst I give you my thoughts. First, it pleases me to see you attired in my late husband's clothes, and even carrying his old sailor's holdall over your shoulder. Thank you so much for all you have done for me. Now, it's my turn to help you. I have here a letter for the harbour-master at Lowestoft Port; he and my hubby were good friends. I am sure he will do his uttermost to assist you. I am aware that you will not take any money from me, so the one thing I can do, and have done, is pack some food plus a few other bits and bobs to take with you. Finally, I have put my foot down with Madge, and when my house is ready for habitation, Ron, Madge and the children will be moving in with me, then I will always have company."

After this, Tom made his farewells and went on his way, promising to return on his way home, but this was a promise he would never keep.

The following day, he reached the port, but, before seeing the harbour-master, he decided to eat the remaining food in the bag. To his surprise, lying in the bottom of the bag was £20 in one-pound notes. The money he hid around his person.

Tom set out to find the harbour-master, and soon found his office. Tom knocked and entered.

Alf, the harbour-master, was sat at his desk. "What can I do for you? If it's work you are after, then there is none to be had, I am sad to say. Search elsewhere, my friend."

"Sir, in my hand is a letter from someone you may recall... Ena?" The envelope was passed over to Alf. Slowly, a broad smile spread across his face as he read the letter.

"Sit down, lad, and let me think about what to do. This is the first time that my dear old friend's wife has ever written to me, so she must think very highly of you indeed. In about a week's time, a Spanish trawler is due to berth. Perez, the captain of this vessel, owes me a few favours. He is a wily creature and breaks the regulations frequently. Most of the time, I turn a blind eye to his escapades. It must be said, though, that every now and then, when he calls on me, I find two bottles of brandy after he has departed. Leave this matter with me. Have you anywhere to stay in the meanwhile? If you have not, it would please me to have you stay with me. I have lived alone since my wife passed away and would be happy with your company for as long as it takes to find you a berth; will that suit you?" Tom acquiesced immediately.

4

The week flew by, each of them content, and long hours were spent reminiscing on various matters. The Spanish ship had docked and would be in port loading and unloading for a few days. At last, they set sail for Madrid. Tom was seasick most of the time, but, despite his ailment, he always completed the chores that were expected of him.

Finally, they berthed in Madrid, and Perez was more than pleased with Tom's efforts. He explained the shortest route to the Alps, warned Tom of the many dangers that he would surely face, then bade him goodbye.

For many weeks, Tom travelled, climbing hills but trying to keep well clear of the mountains, finding even the foothills of the mountains difficult. The first few weeks of his journey had not been too bad; now and then, he found a few villagers who were willing to feed him in exchange for money. Sometimes, he came across lonely shepherds or goatherders, and ate their offerings as they sat around a small fire, sharing whatever they had. However, with his clothing now in tatters, and boots almost worn out, he had been out of food for many days, and was now in total despair.

Desperate for a rest, he lay down and slept, cold and shivering. However, during the night, Tom realized he must walk to keep the cold at bay or die there on the mountain.

Dawn saw Tom cresting yet another hill, and to his astonishment, there in the distance lay a village, the house roofs glistening in the morning sunlight. They were clad in copper surely; could this be the end of his journey? Carefully, Tom made his way down the mountain, fully aware that to rush could prove fatal. Tom was in high spirits, full of hope that he may be able to purchase food plus new clothing as well. At last, Tom reached a pathway of sorts; just a lane. He frowned. This lane had not been maintained for a long time now; that much was obvious to him. Nature had taken over what man had neglected. Trees and bushes were growing in profusion in the roadway, and much was the same with the fields he passed where no crops grew. There was no sign of livestock either, only the birds and bees were evident of life at all! Tom was very troubled with all he had seen up to this point. 'What on earth has happened here?' he wondered. 'Who or what has allowed this to happen?'

A short while later, Tom entered the village. Suddenly, he halted. His mouth hung open - coins of all denominations lay there and amongst them glinted a few precious stones. It was not the treasure hoard that amazed him the most; it was the state of the houses. Doors were hanging off, windows broken, gardens like a wilderness. 'Why?' thought Tom. All this wealth that lay about yet nothing maintained; it was far beyond his comprehension to fathom out.

Old people wandered about the road, some arm in arm, but no young folk whatsoever. Tom was stupefied at what he beheld. He bent down to pick up a precious stone, but, as he did, alarm bells rang in his mind. It was then he recalled the words of old Dennis; "Pick anything up off the road at your peril, for you will never leave this village again!" Tom stood erect, the stone untouched, and walked on. Time after time, he tried to engage with the old people but none would respond. All had a glazed vacant look about them. Tom gave up, and instead, he staggered down the road and met the rising ground. Dennis's words came back to him once more - "Pass through the village, climb the hill, just a short journey to a lovely abode of an old lady named Mary; she will surely bid you welcome!"

As he neared his destination, Tom was once again saddened at what he saw. What at one time had been a fine mansion, Tom mused as he staggered up the long driveway, was nothing more than a dilapidated crumbling ruin. The once-glorious gardens, as they must have been long ago, were returning to forestation. He knocked on the door and was bidden enter. Seated by the fireplace was an old lady of indeterminable years. "Sit down, young man. It has been many years since I last had a visitor. You look worn out; sit and rest for a while. I am afraid I have no food to offer you, however, the fruit trees are laden with their bounty. Help yourself to whatever you need. A little spring lies just beyond the orchard; a good drink it is. Slake your hunger and thirst then we will talk of your journey and whatever you desire. Before you step outside, go to the upper rooms. There, you will find many wardrobes, all full of my late husband's clothes. Help yourself to whatever you want. Also, many pairs of boots abound. Take your choice of them otherwise all will perish in time."

'A very cryptic remark,' thought Tom. 'What can she mean?' He did as instructed and was soon adorned in fresh clothes and boots. He thanked Mary and strode outside to eat his fill of much of the fabulous fruit. As he was eating, he spotted many rabbit droppings. Tom made some snares hoping overnight to trap a couple. He realized that to regain his strength before he returned home, he must have meat. Full at last, his thirst quenched, he re-joined Mary. For hours they spoke; the upshot of their conversation was that Tom would spend a few weeks with her whilst he recuperated and was fit to travel again. Over the following weeks, Mary told Tom of how her husband and herself had come to this haven, which now she called hell.

Her husband was a mercenary general who had fought wars for many years for an Arabian king. Finally, he vanquished the last foe of the said king. Retirement beckoned and Lester, the general, informed his majesty of his intentions. On hearing this, the king enquired what his plans were for the future. "To find a place far away and build a home fit for my Mary and myself, somewhere we can live in peace, and never know hunger, thirst or want ever again. A place that will be free of illness and disease." Those were Lester's wishes. On hearing of his general's desires, the king ordered forth his seer.

"Search amongst the far mountains and find such a place if you can!" A few hours later, the seer returned. "The place you are seeking does indeed exist, many weeks' travel from here, but are you sure, my General, about your wishes? All that you have hoped for will come true, I am sad to say! This village lies in the Alps of Spain. At the moment, it is a peaceful village, with around thirty dwellings, where life and death naturally occur. All this will change once you dwell there all because of your greedy wishes. Indeed, in days to come, wealth itself will have no value there!"

"Take away that creature who has offended my friend! Place him in jail until he rots and may the rats feed on his flesh!" said the king.

5

Two weeks later, Lester and Mary began their long journey. With them were many porters and guides, and ten mules were laden with treasure that Lester had acquired as trophies of war. Also, there was a fabulous coat, a gift from the grateful king: "This coat is made from the best material possible, lined with satin, my friend. As long as you wear it, you will never want for money, but should others wear it, the pockets will be empty. Only for you, or whoever the coat is passed onto, will it function as I say. Goodbye, my friend, and may Allah be with you always."

"So, we arrived in this haven/hell after a long perilous journey," said Mary. "At first, everything was wonderful. Lester employed local labour and built his dream home, and the locals welcomed us with open arms. The village had an inn as well as a small shop and the village doctor was also the midwife and chemist. Now and then, a traveller would call by with wares to sell, so the village was almost self-contained. All that changed very slowly at first, but it gathered pace as the months sped by. People soon realised that if you do not feel hunger or thirst, what is the point of working? First, the inn closed, then the shop shortly after that. No one left the village as they had become accustomed to the easy way of life there. In any case, to leave meant you must stock up with food and clothing, and how could they? The land was no longer farmed, the shop was shut, no travellers called… they were trapped! Most of the villagers came to hate us and I can understand why now. I feel sad for them and myself; this is surely hell on earth! My last visitor came about forty years ago. He must have been about your age. He stopped with us for many weeks, and, like yourself, he was worn out. What was his name now?"

"Could his name be Dennis?" Tom enquired. "I met this old man a few months ago and long did he reminisce about this place. That is the reason I have made this journey; I had to find out if this place really existed. This is my pilgrimage, but what I have seen here up to now has been a massive let-down to me. Yes, I have seen wealth lying about here, enough to last me many lifetimes if I chose to pick it up. I have learned a valuable lesson though - gold and other precious metals do not feed you; only the land can do that."

Over the next few weeks, Tom regained his strength. He and Mary talked long into the nights, so during the last few days of his visit, Mary became more and more morose. Something was troubling her. Mary told Tom that he must leave the following day and she explained why. "Beyond the mountain that towers over this valley is a glacier. It moves imperceptibly and very soon it will push the mountain away. In the past few weeks, there have been small falls of rock, and the rumbling from the mountain has been ever constant. Soon, the whole valley will disappear as though it never existed, so that is why you must leave! Pack as many clothes and boots as you can carry. Take plenty of fruit as well; you will need it, but do not discard the pips or seeds. Take them home and all will grow. However, on the day you die, so will the trees."

"What about yourself, Mary? What are your plans?"

"I intend to stay here to witness this vile hell wiped from the face of the Earth!" By noon the following day, Tom was partway up the mountain that he had descended six weeks before. Suddenly, a mighty roar was heard. The far mountain had collapsed as Mary had forecast, and, within minutes, the valley was buried in what seemed to be 100 feet or more of rocky debris. This was followed by torrents of water from the glacier and within the hour, the valley was a raging river! Tom turned and continued his walk, shocked and confused by the events.

After many months, he emerged from the Alps, not in Spain but Portugal. Several weeks later, Tom was still searching the dock hoping to find a working passage home. It took a few weeks to find a ship, however, the only one docking in England was going to Liverpool. Of course, this meant another long walk, so it was three weeks later before he arrived home, just about able to stand, and with his feet wrapped in whatever he could find. The first person he came across was his own son toiling in the field.

6

Don was clearly agitated, which was obvious to his mother. "I must be leaving soon; Jackson will be waiting for me." Sarah gave a rueful smile; it was her son's big day - it was the day of the county show! Don had spent more and more time with Jenny. Sarah spoke to her son; "Do not expect too much from the horse today. Both you and Jackson have tried your best, but you must understand what the farmer told you. Jenny has very little chance of winning anything at all. I wish you well, of course."

Don exploded with anger. "Can't win?!" he raged. "I'll show them!" Off he set to the farm, musing to himself - could he improve the horse any more?

Arriving at the farm, Don was aware that Jenny was in harnesses, ready to be backed into the shafts of a trap. They soon had Jenny buckled up and ready to go. Don climbed onto the passenger seat. Jackson was shaking his head. "Tha canna sit there, lad," he said in a glum voice. "For the first time in years, yon t'owd hag has said she is coming, so there!"

"Where can I sit?" asked Don anxiously. "Trap will only seat two!"

"In the only perch left, on t'owd 'oss's back. Mount up, cos here comes my jailer - vindictive ol' bag spoiling my day." Jane, the farmer's wife, strode across the farmyard. Jackson could not believe his eyes - there was his wife wearing a new coat, hat and dress, and with makeup on her face! He just stared, dumbfounded. She looked twenty years younger. He sat there mesmerised. "Ah tha gonna gis a hand up, tha old fool? I canna climb up on me own!" Jackson duly helped her up, and, with a grunt and a silent curse, off they set. Don was thinking to himself that he had the best seat of all.

It was more than six miles to the county show-ground, so it took the best part of two hours. That the old horse was dusty and tired did not need stating. They set about cleaning Jenny as best they could. Don was aware that other entrants in the horse show were arriving in horse boxes. He watched the first few unload; his face crestfallen.

Jenny and Don walked around the parade area. The old horse was very tired from the morning's excursion, and her head hung low. Don wished the parade was over; here he was leading a tired old horse with not a chance of any prize at all. Jackson was fuming over the cat calls, jeers and snide remarks from the crowd when they saw Jenny. It only wanted some tinder to ignite his fury! With fists clenched, he stared balefully at the onlookers. The spark came in the form of one of his neighbouring farmers, Jack Straw. Now Jack was a big burly genial type of man. He enjoyed banter - a bit of fun. Jack approached Jackson and commented, "Thars a brave man, Jackson, showing that tired old nag. Is it best tha can do?" He winked at the onlookers. "Tha got some guts indeed."

Jane, also fuming, heard these remarks. "Jack Straw," she said, "thar are nothing but a big bag of wind and piss! My man is a better farmer and a far better man than thee! Regarding thy observations that our 'oss 'as no chance of winning anything, I will bet you £20 that my horse wins a prize, you bag of shit!"

Jack was not a gambling man. He detested any form of wager. However, if he turned down the bet, he knew he would look very foolish indeed. "Very well, Mrs Jackson, I accept yon bet on one condition - that no attempt has been made or will be made to bribe the judges." Jane and Jackson went very quiet. They had forgotten that Jack Straw's brother-in-law was the top horse judge here today.

Embarrassed and red in the face, Jane replied, "The bet is on!" In tears, she walked away, a month's housekeeping placed on a stupid bet.

Jackson could take no more. He stood up to Jack Straw, saying, "You big bastard, you have upset my wife! Let's settle this man to man; take thee coat off, scumbag!" Jack was at least six inches taller and a stone heavier than Jackson, and he did not want to fight. His attempts at having a bit of fun had backfired on him. He was not afraid of fighting Jackson; on the contrary, he was afraid of hurting him.

"Look, I've had enough of a tussle wi' thy missus; ahm pleased she none my wife. Let things simmer down, eh? Enjoy the show!"

A great roar emitted from Jackson. "First you take the piss out me 'oss and now you've caused tears to flow from my wife!" He added, "At least I know that my boys are all from the same stable! Can you say the same about yours?" No one was allowed to talk to Jack Straw like that and get away without a pasting. He ripped his coat off and strode to Jackson. By this time, the parade had stopped, and all the handlers and horses were looking over the fence waiting for battle to commence!

The first blow, a mighty punch that caught him right in the face, knocked Jackson down. The Straw-man (Jack Straw's nickname) strode up and said, "Ah tha all rate, old man?" in a very concerned voice. "Ah never ment to hit thee hard!"

Jackson got up, spat out two loose teeth and bellowed, "Round Two!" The area was packed with spectators, horse show forgotten. The fight continued for a few minutes more, then Jackson caught the Straw-man a wicked blow to the stomach. Straw-man lay prone on the turf for a few seconds then raised himself on his elbows, grinned at Jackson and asked, "Tha's had enough, Jackson?"

The old farmer could see that Jack was laughing with contentment. Jackson agreed, "Yes, I've had enough."

"Give a man a hand then," the younger farmer said. As soon as both of them were on their feet, they hugged each other. The crowd erupted with applause. These two stalwarts were to remain friends for the rest of their lives. "Men!" Jane said in disgust. "Boys that have grown in height, but still contain the mentality of children." Her heart softened somewhat when she thought of Jackson; very little give in the old fool. 'My knight in shining armour, defending my honour?' She smiled ruefully to herself. The armour is getting very rusty and the knight is approaching daybreak. Lost in thought, she failed to register the loud applause from the parade ground. 'They can't have announced the winners yet!' She rose to her feet and walked over to the parade ground, which was empty but for one horse - Jenny!

Unbeknownst to Jackson or Jane, over the past few weeks, Don had taught Jenny to do certain skills. A few minutes earlier, he had whispered in the horse's ear, "Jackson and Straw-man have put on a show; now it's our turn, lass." It's debatable whether Jenny had understood the speech from her friend but she seemed to shake her head in agreement! All the other horses had left the parade ring, so Don began to coax Jenny into showing her skills. He stood in front of the horse and stamped his right foot. Jenny immediately rolled onto her right side. Don then stamped his left foot and Jenny completely rolled over. Then Don gave a slight jump and landed, stamping both feet! The old horse turned onto her back and began waving her hooves in turn! By this time, Jane had joined the throng that was watching this spectacle. Tears were streaming down her face. This was the horse she had rescued many years ago after Jenny's mother had passed on. Don pointed to the sky, and Jenny rose to fantastic applause. With the little stick that he carried, he tapped Jenny's knees. The horse immediately sank to the floor, resting on her knees, allowing Don to mount her very easily. They trotted around the parade ground then Don raised himself upright, arms akimbo, riding a full circuit around the ground; more applause. Then Jackson appeared, his face very stony!

He took the lead from Don then led Jenny away. Don was mortified; what had he done wrong? Jenny could have performed many more skills yet. Jane, observing her husband's behaviour, was perplexed. Don and the horse were giving a wonderful show. Jackson arrived at her side and stated, "We are going home."

Jane tried to point out that the results of the show had not been announced yet. "For once in your life, listen to what I say!" he snorted at her. "As tha forgot the vows you made long ago?!" Mortified, Jane fell silent. This was a man she scarcely recognised.

"I'll wait by the trap," she replied.

"Then thar'll wait a long time," roared Jackson. "We are walking home!" They set off on their long walk home, stopping at least every mile or so. Not a word was spoken during the whole journey, which was far longer than anticipated. Arriving back at the farm, Jackson, in a gruff voice, thanked Don for his efforts and bade the bewildered lad goodbye!

'Time to visit Joe,' Straw-man mused. (Joe was his brother-in-law and head judge of the show). Striding up to the judges' tent, he was aware of the sign in front of the entrance - "Do not enter without permission". Straw-man went straight in. "Nah then, Jack," said one of the minor judges. "Can't tha read notice?" The official felt a huge hand take a very loose grip of his throat.

"Listen, fish-face, it doesn't say on notice who gives permission, so am asking thee, is it all rate for me to cum in?" Straw-man was assured he could enter.

He went over to Joe. "'As tha done prize list yet, Joe?" The judge informed him that he was first and second in the show and this year he would be presented with a brand-new silver cup, yet to be engraved. Jack took a look at the cup. "Ah don't want that tat; it means more work for Nellie to keep clean." The judges were bemused. "We have nothing else for first prize, Jack."

"Then give me a gold rosette," he snarled at them. "Wot's Jackson's 'oss won?" he asked them.

"That old bag of bones? If there had been 30 entrants, at best, Jenny would have been placed 31st."

"Does tha know Ted Sloan by any chance, Joe?"

"Aye, he's local undertaker."

"Just to save Ted a bit of hassle, why dunt tha pop round for a fittin'? It may come in handy soon, especially for thee! I have set me heart on Jenny, broken-down mare she may be, winning a prize today. It would fair rile me if Jackson won nowt, dos tha understand me?" Straw-man quietly asked.

"All the prizes have been awarded, Jack, and that list cannot be altered!"

"Have I asked thee to alter placings?" Jack thundered at them. "I'm not a judge; you lot are meant to be!"

They discussed the problem in the judges' tent. Forty minutes and two crates of beer later, a solution was agreed. Straw-man spoke; "So, we are agreed with the inscription then?" Hands were shaken all round and Straw-man left.

Jenny had been bedded down for the night, with extra oats, etc. Jackson walked to his home. He had quietened down somewhat but was still very upset. He had berated himself remorselessly, very angry that it had taken a relative stranger to point out the old horse's needs. Entering the kitchen, he noted Jane had prepared a wonderful meal. Down he sat himself and just picked at the meal, where normally he would have wanted more! Jane, for once, never said a word to her husband; she just observed. Jackson rose. "Ahm going to bed, lass; see thee soon." Jane tidied up, set the table for breakfast and joined her husband in bed.

"Right," she said, "let's be knowing what has caused thee such grief." So, he told her; he also admitted that he had spent a large amount of money and would she please understand why he had spent most of their resources. "You old fool, it is something you should have done years ago!" She hugged him for many a long moment and then made plans for the next day, but like all plans, they do not always work out!

Before the cockerel had welcomed the new day, Jackson was walking to the stables. Jenny heard him coming and, in her way, groaned, still very tired from yesterday. 'Looks like a full day's work today,' she thought. Jackson opened the stable doors, put the halter on Jenny and led her into the farmyard. 'Tracks and chains next,' thought Jenny, but, to her surprise, he led her down the lane. The old horse was puzzled. After walking for about ten minutes, they stopped at a gate that led to a small meadow; a meadow that Jackson had intended cutting for feed for the coming winter, however, having cut the fields belonging to Silas, he did not need any more hay, did he? The meadow was damp with morning dew, full of daisies, buttercups and other varied flora. Jenny's nostrils flared at the wonderful aroma. 'If only I could stay here,' Jenny thought in her own way, 'wouldn't it be fantastic?' To her surprise, Jackson led her in, removed the halter, said "Happy retirement!" then closed the gate and walked back home.

Pottering about the farmyard whilst waiting for his sons to finish their breakfast, Jackson knew that they had got their way. For the past year or so, they had pleaded with him, "Dad, you must modernise otherwise the farm will not pay." Resolutely, he smiled to himself. He had one more card to play.

"Morning, Dad!" they called in unison. "Top field needs ploughing, hay to move and other jobs, alright, Dad?" Tony, the eldest, went to prepare Jenny for the day's work. He came running back within minutes. "Dad, Dad, 'oss's gone!"

Jackson gave a nod. "Aye, tow'd 'oss has pulled her last plough. She retired as of this morning."

"How can we plough the fields wi'out 'oss?" they asked.

"Well," said their dad, "wi' three fine strapping lads like you lot, who needs an 'oss?! Two can pull plough an' tother can guide from back shouting mush or whatever."

The sons were gobsmacked. "That's no good, Dad," they chorused. Their dad went quiet for a few moments. "Mind you, there is always plan B. All three of you go to Straw-man's for the day to learn to drive a tractor!"

Jane was clutching the sink, her ribs aching, convulsed

with laughter at the sight of the four men in the yard, three of them her sons, who looked to be playing ring-a-ring of roses. They were laughing and whooping with delight. The sons had tried to pull Dad into the circle but he was having none of it! It was plain that Jackson was berating them, telling the sons to go away. He lost his temper, and, with a well-placed boot, caught one of them up the backside. They scattered and then proceeded to Straw-man's farm.

Jane prepared breakfast for her hubby and herself, knowing he would soon be in. A few minutes later, hands washed and boots cleaned, he sat down to eat. Jane, for once, joined him. Jane did all the talking, while Jackson did all the grunting in reply to various questions. With breakfast done, he sat down to a leisurely read in his old armchair. Jane washed the pots then carried on cooking. Suddenly, they heard a clatter of hooves in the farmyard. It was Straw-man!

Straw-man unhitched his horse from Jackson's trap and strode into the kitchen. "Morning, Jane, Jackson," said Jack. "Whilst I was going to the show-ground this morn, I thought I may as well bring your trap back." Jackson thanked him for his help and bade him take a seat and join them for a cup of tea.

After a few minutes, Straw-man placed £20 on the table. "For you, Jane; I have paid me bet!"

"Do you mean to tell me Jenny won a prize? Anyroad, I laid that bet in false pretences."

"I know what you and Jackson did, trying to bribe the judges! And forgetting yon top judge married mah sister. Of course, he told me; why do you think I placed the bet? Joe had already told me that your old nag had no chance of winning at all!"

"Still," Jane replied, "being as we both tried to cheat, call it a draw?"

"On one condition," Jack said. "Put that money towards helping the old and poor in the village."

"I'll do no such thing!" Jane said angrily.

Jack, unusually for him, answered, "It's been an open secret for many years that I just want to help a little." Jack rose to go, but as he opened the door, he turned and said, "In back of trap there is a little parcel..."

Jackson stretched and yawned. "Ah go an' put t'owd trap in back o' barn; it will be a long time afore it's used again, if ever." Jane nodded to her hubby in agreement; that her man needed help was obvious to her. Jane and Jackson pulled and tugged and eventually, the trap was placed where he had specified. As they were walking away, Jane remembered Straw-man informing them that there was a little parcel for them in the trap. Jackson climbed into the vehicle and picked up a nondescript parcel, tied with twine and wrapped in old newspapers. He showed it to Jane and they both commented, "No expense spared then!" They made their way back to the farmhouse, put the parcel on the table and brewed a pot of tea.

"Ah suppose the parcel has to be opened," said Jane. All the fabulous wrapping was removed with due reverence and slung on the floor. They opened the box. To say they were overawed would be a vast understatement. Neither spoke for a few minutes. Then Jackson said, "There is only one place for this!" Jane put her coat on.

"Morning, Mrs Pepper," Jane said. "Is Don in? This old fool of mine has come to apologise again."

Sarah made them both welcome. "Please come in. Don will be home for his lunch in about twenty minutes, so I'll make a pot of tea." Jane gazed around the frugal little home. It was spotless. This, she thought, was a good caring lady. They had their cups of tea and spoke of things in general. After half an hour had passed, Jane rose. "You'll have to forgive me, Mrs Pepper, but we have to be going. This little parcel we are leaving is for Don. Also, I had forgotten that my three sons are working at Jack Straw's farm today, and I have baked too much. It would please me if you would accept this apple pie."

Don came in about ten minutes later. Sarah informed him of the visitors and pointed to the parcel. "That is yours from them both." Once Don had eaten his lunch, he opened the parcel; the contents amazed him. He could not utter a sound. Sarah was puzzled. What had caught her son's attention? Then he showed his mum. Sarah, with a tremor in her voice, read the inscription on the trophy. "For the finest display by any shire horse, this cup is awarded (in perpetuity) to Jenny, owned by Jackson and trained by Mr Donald Pepper."

Sarah was very proud of her son. If only Tom could see this, he too would be overjoyed. 'I wonder where Tom is now,' thought Sarah. Don didn't say a word about the silver cup. Too full of emotion, he left the table, donned his jacket and returned to work. He would treasure that silver cup for the rest of his life.

In the years that followed, when he was left the inn by Silas Mimms, he became landlord of the inn. That trophy was proudly displayed in a glass cabinet on a high shelf. Over the years, many people commented on how well-polished it was. A few even expressed a wish to handle it. However, this was always met with the same answer - "NEVER!"

7

Sarah had plans of her own for the day of the horse show. She had noticed that Don usually called on Silas at roughly a set time. She quizzed her son as to why he had to go and visit Silas. "It's just to allow Mr Mimms to do his various shopping needs and he needs someone there in case the doctor comes early." Sarah was puzzled.

"Why does Mrs Mimms not do the shopping? She always 'as done as far as I can recall, and for what reason is the doctor calling?"

"No idea," replied Don.

Sarah packed a few things in her bag and strode down to the rear entrance of the inn. Silas answered her knock on the door. "Don's not coming today, Mr Mimms, so I have come to help you. Tell me what you need doing."

"Mrs Pepper," said Silas, "I do not want any help, thank you!" Silas blocked the doorway; he had no intention of allowing this woman into his home.

"Get out of my way, you stupid man! I am coming in!" So shocked was Silas that he immediately gave Sarah access.

Sarah walked into Silas's kitchen and cringed at the mess. This place had not had a woman's touch for some time. Pots lay unwashed, there were piles of dirty laundry on the floor and the food was rank by the smell of it. "Mr Mims," said Sarah, "light the copper."

"I will do no such thing, Mrs Pepper, and will you please leave now?!"

"Get out of my way, you old fool! I will light the copper myself." Silas could see he was beaten; in truth, he had no fight left in him. What with his wife's illness, trying to run the inn, and doing the cleaning and cooking as best he could, he was completely worn out.

"I'll fetch the kindling and light the copper, Mrs Pepper." 'Anything for peace and quiet,' he thought to himself. Sarah swept by him and made her way to the stairs. A feeble protest from Silas was ignored. As she walked up the stairs, the foul damp atmosphere hit her and Sarah grimaced. She found Mrs Mimms lying in her bed, gasping for breath, curtains drawn, certainly very ill. The first thing Sarah did was to open the curtains and windows fully. Sarah spoke to Mrs Mimms and told her she was here to help. Back downstairs, Sarah went into the bar. She spotted what she was looking for - two middle-aged men having a drink. "I want a hand with moving things upstairs; will you help me, please?" The men looked at Silas for confirmation that it was alright to proceed. Silas just shrugged his shoulders. Dan and Mick followed Sarah upstairs.

"First, roll up that carpet, take it outside and drape it over the wall." Dan and his mate did as they were told, then Sarah followed them down. "Next, come into the parlour. That black leather chair - please put it into the bedroom by the window. Finally, when that is done, I want this carpet beating for at least an hour, and keep turning it! When I am satisfied it's as clean as you can get it, take it back into the bedroom and re-lay it. During the course of the beating, refreshments will be provided, and for the rest of the day." Silas just groaned. Sarah knew it would take many visits to get the inn to a reasonable standard of cleanliness.

Back into the bar she went. "Mr Mimms, have you got a ladder?" Silas told her that he had. "Right then, clean those bedroom windows - now!"

"What about the bar?" Silas asked.

"How many are there in the pub now? None."

As instructed, Silas cleaned the windows, but to his satisfaction, not to Sarah's. "You call them clean? Do them again and get into the corners! When I am pleased with the outside, come and clean inside."

"Right," said Silas.

Sarah helped Mrs Mimms into the leather chair. The curtains had been taken down by then and the bedding was stripped and placed in the copper which by now was boiling. Fresh bedding, slightly damp, was found and the bed was remade. She dusted and cleaned the rest of the room as best she could with the tackle she had. Back downstairs, she removed the bedding from the copper, put it through the mangle then hung it out to dry. Martha gazed contentedly through the clean windows, watching Dan and Mick stagger up the drive, arms linked about each other for support. They had earned their drink. 'Silas has done me proud,' she thought as she put down her now empty cup and snuggled back into the armchair, mulling over the day's events. Clean windows! Clean curtains! Clean bedding! Sheer bliss. The gentle breeze wafted through the open windows. She had never felt so content in months. Martha was well aware that this was a false illusion. She had overheard the doctor and Silas talking about her illness. The doctor had told her husband that it was only a matter of months, even with the best of care. Martha recalled the past hour. Sarah had pulled up a chair alongside, gently holding her hand. Silas had come to ask if they wanted a drink. Martha requested a hot toddy, and asked, "Will you join me?" but Sarah declined.

The three of them talked for over an hour. Silas had poured himself a large whisky, even though he did not normally drink. When she was ready, Sarah made her farewells and went home, promising to come back most days. Silas left Martha and went back to the bar to count the day's takings, re-stock as required, and clean the tap room ready for the night trade. He looked at the till; takings were very low, yet the amount of beer consumed was very high. He was rather remorseful for a while. Then he could feel a wide beaming smile coming on! If that is all it takes to keep Martha content, he would do the same every day. Martha had drifted into a quiet nap, dreaming of the days long ago, looking through these same windows, watching their son Richard chasing rabbits and suchlike in the meadow by the side of the wood. He never caught any, of course, but it was wonderful watching him. Then came the day he left to join the army and fight for his country in the war to end all wars, as it was called. He never returned. Killed on the Somme. Neither she nor Silas had ever got over that dreadful news.

Sarah had suggested, in a gentle tone, that it would be beneficial for his wife if he moved into his son's bedroom and there was no objection from Silas. He could see sense in what Sarah had said. So, at bedtime, Silas made sure that Martha was comfortable, closing windows and curtains, then pulling blankets up to Martha's chin. He then put himself to bed, relishing the wonderfully soft, clean, crisp sheets. It was the first time since his son had left home all those years ago that he had entered this room. Silas lay in bed, gazing around the room. All Richard's toys lay there. He vowed not to go to sleep if he could help it. He lay there, trying to stay awake. Eventually, tiredness overcame him and he drifted off. Silas dreamt of the days when he took Richard to the woods, first as a young child and latterly as a fine upstanding young man. Taking Richard down to the wood was pure joy. He recalled the time when he had explained to his son that this wood was a sanctuary for wildlife. No creature was to be hunted there. All they could remove from this area was the dead, diseased fallen trees. This was insisted on by the first Mimms that settled there. Indeed, there was a covenant written into the deeds.

Silas was enjoying this dream; in it, he was holding Richard's hand. Then he heard tap, tap, tap, tap… "Ah, a woodpecker," he told his son! He let go of his son's hand to point out where the tapping was coming from, but when he turned to take Richard's hand again, the hand had vanished! He searched all over but could not find the boy. Tap, tap, tap, tap… Silas cursed the bird… tap, tap, tap… He awoke with a start and realised it was Martha tapping on the wall. He hurriedly dressed and went to his wife. "Sorry to disturb you, but can you please draw back the curtains and open the windows for me? Also, help me into the leather chair. I can hear the birds singing and I would like to watch them."

8

Martha lasted a few months longer than the doctor had forecast. "It is due to the wonderful ministrations that you both gave her," said the doctor when she finally passed. "Without your help and Sarah's, Martha would have died months ago." Then the doctor left.

Sarah turned to Silas; "Would you like me to tell Ted? I can also visit the vicar, if you wish." He just nodded, too tearful to talk. Within the hour, Ted and the vicar arrived, one to measure, the other to give condolences. Over the following days, arrangements were made for the interment and the date was set for ten days after her death. The inn had been closed shortly before her passing and remained closed until a week after her funeral.

Two days before the burial, Silas heard noises coming from the garden. Dan and Mick were cutting hedges and grass, and weeding the flower beds, etc. The garden looked immaculate. He went out to thank them, and to tell them there would be no free beer until after the funeral.

"It is not being done for you," Dan said in a very harsh tone. "Keep the free beer; it's being done in the memory of a wonderful lady!"

It was a very small funeral. Neither Martha nor Silas had any close relatives. There was just Silas, Sarah and her two children. As they entered the church, Silas noted that Mick and Dan, heads bowed, both had razor cuts on their faces.

It was obvious that the pair of them had done their best to look clean and suitably dressed for the occasion. Silas gave a brief nod to them, then followed the coffin to the front of the church. Just a short service, that's what Silas had requested.

Sarah continued to visit Silas about two or three times a week, and often, after cleaning duties, they would share a light breakfast.

The weeks rolled by... winter, spring and the onset of summer. Early in May, whilst working in the kitchen, Sarah noticed an old man talking to her son in the field. The old man kept pointing, telling Don what to do. As if her son needed advice about the land! The old man left Don and started to walk to her home. He tapped on the door, and Sarah, being polite, invited him in for a cup of tea. He removed his hat and the very, very tatty old coat and said, "My name is Dennis, Mrs Pepper."

Sarah was totally amazed at the transformation before her eyes. This old man had passed through her door looking like a vagrant; his coat was not even fit for rags! And now, here stood this dapper person, dressed in the best fashion available. Why, he even smelled of aftershave and cologne! With shaking hands, she asked him to sit down, brewed tea and produced fresh baked scones. Dennis was very content and seemed to enjoy his meal. "Have you heard from Tom lately?" he asked.

"How do you know my husband?"

"Tom will be home in a few months, carrying great treasure," he added hastily, "but not treasure as you know it."

"I don't give a damn about the treasure! All I want is my husband back!" Sarah was getting very angry; all this talk about treasure indeed!

Things were quiet for a while then Dennis spoke; "I did not mean to cause offence, Mrs Pepper, I do apologise." Sarah calmed down at last. At length, Dennis said, "That tattered old coat, I will leave it here for Tom; it needs to be cleaned and patched. I am sure he will welcome it." With that said, Dennis left.

Sarah gingerly pulled up the coat. "That is to be dumped; no way can that be cleaned!"

Her daughter, young Sarah, had obtained a position in a small dressmaking shop and she was expecting her home for lunch. Apparently, she was doing very well. She had introduced new styles in ladies' dresses, and, to the astonishment of her boss, they were selling like hotcakes! Her employer, a Mrs Smith, was aware that if Sarah progressed in this way, she would be leaving for one of the top fashion chains.

Sarah came through the door, sat down and ate her frugal lunch. She had placed herself on a very strict diet! Lunch over, her mother pointed out the pile of rags in the corner. Sarah told her daughter about the visit of Dennis. Young Sarah looked at the rags with disdain, then her curiosity got the better of her. "Mum," she said, "the lining of this coat is barely damaged; it is made of the purest silk! And the cloth itself is a wonderful material. Maybe if we removed the lining and give that a cool wash, the rest of the coat can be soaked in the dolly tub. Much possing will be required." Her daughter had finished her lunch, picking and prodding at the food. 'Becoming quite a lady,' Sarah thought. 'It's wonderful that she has done so well at the shop. I just wish she would drop some of the airs and graces that she has picked up.' It was understandable in a way. Most of the younger ladies (and older ones!) would only discuss their needs with young Sarah.

Don often teased his sister for her ladylike ways, and Sarah, in return, would point out that he had made a success of becoming the village idiot! 'Always plenty of banter,' their mother thought.

Over the next few days and many washes later, the lining of the old coat was carefully replaced. To stitch the rest of the coat together took nearly a week of their time!

A lovely job had been made of the coat, she mused, even though it resembled a pile of clean rags in her opinion.

9

Don was working in the fields gathering crops. Sarah often watched her son through the kitchen window. That he was a wonderful son was obvious to all that knew him. Suddenly, a most dreadful sight came into view. Don was standing talking to the worst tramp she had ever seen in her life! 'I do wish Don wouldn't talk to or even mix with vermin,' she mused. As she finished washing the dishes, she glanced up, and, to her amazement, she saw Don put his arms around the filthy bedraggled man!

As she started to wipe the dishes, something clicked. The plate she was drying fell to the floor and she bolted out the door and ran up the lane as fast as she could! Her daughter had heard the plate smash on the floor, looked up sharply and saw the back of her mother darting through the door.

'What now? What is Mum up to? I will wipe the rest of the pots,' she thought. She looked through the kitchen window and saw that Don was in an embrace with a filthy old tramp. Her mother had just arrived on the scene and young Sarah was astonished to see that her mum was pulling Don away from this creature, and even more astonished to see her jump into the tramp's arms! Another plate smashed on the floor, all ladylike pretensions forgotten. Young Sarah, her long skirts held up in one hand, showed more speed and agility than her mother had shown. As she ran, she screamed, "DAD, DAD, DAD!" Her father was home again.

They hugged each other for a few minutes then Sarah realised that when they held Tom, he was wincing with pain. She gazed down at his feet - both feet were bleeding. She was horrified to see that his feet were covered with nothing more than dock leaves, long grass and tied around with rags from his clothing. How long he had walked with this was truly amazing. It was certain that he could not walk another step; somehow, he had to be carried home.

Jackson was working in the next field harvesting potatoes with his eldest son. He had seen the tramp approaching Don, then mother and daughter racing up the lane. 'Tom's home; that's marvellous, private party, keep thee nose out, Jackson,' he thought. As he turned his back to the field, he heard sharp cries of anguish coming from the two ladies. 'Somat amiss here; time to poke nose in, owd lad.' With that thought in his mind, he made his way through a gap in the hedge. One glance at Tom's condition told him more than a thousand words ever could. He spun around, ran back to the field, stopped the tractor and told his eldest son, "Take tractor back 'ome, bring t'owd trap outa back and bring it back here!"

Jane heard the tractor chugging onto the farmyard. 'What on earth is going on?' she wondered. Hurrying across the yard and talking to her son, she made him wait for a few minutes to give her time to parcel up a few things that Sarah may need to help her man. A couple of bedsheets were quickly torn into makeshift bandages, etc., then she added a sandwich and Jackson's old bedroom slippers - 'Worn out anyway,' she mused, 'so the old fool can always buy some more!' The son took the parcel and put it into the hastily rigged-up trap. Jane would have liked nothing better than to go too, but she understood that Sarah would wish to look after Tom herself. The tractor roared out of the farmyard as fast as it could go. Sarah had calmed down somewhat and gave her children instructions. "Don, fill the copper and get out the tin bath. Sarah, you fetch some blankets, clothes, etc." She and Jackson did their best to make Tom comfortable despite his protestations. He gave up arguing, realising that it was a waste of time.

Sarah tried to remove the small bag that Tom was clutching fiercely. "NO!" yelled Tom. "That bag holds my treasure!" Tom was placed in the trap and taken the short journey home. Jackson's son had shown his dad the little parcel that Jane had sent. "The old hag!" he said to himself. "The old cow! Giving away my slippers!" He thought about taking them back, but if he did, all hell would be let loose.

Jackson's feet were larger than Tom's, but with Tom's feet being badly swollen, they might just fit. "'Ere, Tom, put these on." With some effort, he managed to get them onto his feet. Tom gratefully thanked his friend. Tom insisted on walking to the cottage, but Sarah, equally, insisted on giving her support to him.

Don, as instructed by his mum, had placed a chair on the path just outside the door. "Sit there," Sarah told her husband. "First, your feet are to be put in to soak, then your hair will be cut! After that, you are going to have a long hot bath in front of the fire, and, if I think it needs it, another bath! Any objections?" Tom wearily nodded, too tired to argue.

Young Sarah picked up two carrots and a crust of bread. "Don, let us go and see Jenny and maybe walk through Silas's wood." Don insisted on staying but Sarah continued, "Don, use what little common sense you have left. Dad walked up the path; yes, he's tired. Most of his hair must come off, his feet need a long soak, then Mum will sit him in the bath, possibly changing the water at least once. Can you imagine Mum wanting us around? Come on!"

As they approached the meadow gate, Jenny came to greet them. A few months ago, Jenny would have charged down the field to greet them; now she plodded slowly. Don knew that the old horse would not survive long at all. They fed her the tit-bits. In return, Jenny nuzzled both of them. After about half an hour, they said their goodbyes. All this was observed by Jackson. His face was very sad. Jackson was torn between letting the animal live out her natural life in pain and discomfort or sending for Albert, the local vet. His mind would be made up over the next few days.

Silas had spotted Sarah and Don as they passed the inn. Waves were exchanged. Don had told his sister about Silas's rule concerning the small wood, and she was very content with that. Don pointed out the seat that Silas had made long ago when he and Martha were courting. Silas had told Don, "Under no circumstances are you to remove that old seat. I am aware that it is in a very poor condition but it holds many wonderful memories for me." As they left the wood, Silas was waiting for them; he had heard that Tom was back. They told Silas that there was no doubt Tom would visit the inn when he was fit to walk. They explained about his feet and lack of proper footwear. Don noticed that Dan and Mick were renovating the old barn, taking out rotten windows and doorways, repointing, etc. Silas became aware of Don looking at the barn. "It badly needed doing. When that work is concluded, that rough pair start on the house. That is, if I can get them to spare time for me! Others have noticed how good they are getting at this renovation lark. More and more people are using their services. In consequence, they are doing less and less for me. My takings have taken a fall, I can tell you!" Grinning, he turned away. When they arrived home, Sarah told them, "Dad's fast asleep, so you'll see him in the morning."

Joe Platts had been keeping a very watchful eye on Mick and Dan. Joe was the only recognised builder in this and the surrounding villages. There were quite a few odd-job men, of that he was well aware. In fact, when they needed any bricks or timber, Joe happily supplied them, at a reasonable profit, of course! Mick and his mate had often worked for Joe on a casual basis - very good workers but not very bright in Joe's eyes. Okay for digging drains, foundations, mixing bulk concrete, etc., but no sooner had he paid them, than the pair scrambled to the local boozer. Joe was amazed at the quality of the work they were turning out. Where they had started repointing, it was obvious that their initial attempts bordered on the amateur. However, as their work progressed, it improved by leaps and bounds! Now Joe, in his late fifties, was not ready to retire. True, he was turning work down lately. He just did not relish having to graft anymore. The ideal world for Joe was that he would do the tendering, invoicing, books, etc., and leave the actual physical work to others. He believed he had found what he wanted!

Over the course of the next few days, always during lunch breaks at the inn, Joe laid out what his plans would hopefully be for the future - a partnership for the three of them. Neither Dan nor Mick could work out why Joe was giving such generous terms, when all they could impart was their muscle. Still, the details were agreed and the next step was a visit to a solicitor to draw up a formal binding agreement. An appointment was made for the following week and, all being well, the partnership could commence shortly. However, Joe had picked a solicitor who had a very dubious reputation to say the least. Neither Mick nor his mate was aware of this and the three of them were ushered into the office of Josiah Kemp, a very fat gentleman, who seemed to display a permanent sneer. He bade Joe be seated. Mick and Dan were not offered a chair. Mick began to go red in the face at this snub but kept quiet. "Am I to understand that you wish to go into partnership with these men?!" He took out his handkerchief and held it to his nose looking very disdainfully at Mick and Dan. "Really, have you lost use of your faculties, Mr Platts?" Mick could stand it no more. With a lunge, he grabbed hold of Josiah and shook him like a terrier shakes a rat. "One more word from you, you fat twat, and I'll give you something for lunch - a knuckle sandwich!" Dan and Mick stormed out, slamming the door behind them. Joe sat there stony-faced.

"Call the police!" Josiah shouted to his clerk. "I will have them jailed for assault and threats!"

"I will leave you," Joe said quietly.

"Mr Platts, you will of course be submitted an account for this day's work and I expect swift payment!"

"You fat fraud, I have no intention of paying you one penny!"

"You will be sued; of that I can assure you."

Joe, talking softly, replied, "Do you recall when you overcharged me by a vast amount some years ago? Can you remember how many widows and orphans you have robbed?"

"I will sue you for every penny you have!" screamed Josiah.

Joe just smiled. "Opened your morning mail yet?" he asked.

"None of your damn business," came the reply.

"In that case, I will give you a copy of a letter that I received last week informing me that in reply to my letter, the Law Society are coming today!"

Joe knew where to find the two reprobates - in the nearest boozer! As Joe entered, Dan said, "Tha's no need to tell us, partnership's off!"

"You could not be more wrong! It is stronger than ever. You behaved just as I'd hoped you would. I have been after that cheating swindler for a long time. The evidence I have given to the Law Society means that the least he can hope for is being disbarred!"

"But, but..." Mick exclaimed, "he had sent for the police... I will be arrested and jailed!"

"Why, what did you do?" Joe asked innocently. "All I saw was you shaking his hand; thanking him for his help."

"Dan heard me threaten him, didn't you, Dan?" Dan started rubbing his ears. "Not heard a damn thing all day; must go to the doctors." They all grinned.

"Right," said Joe, "sup up. We are off to John Kirk's; as solicitors go, he's a decent bloke." By late afternoon, with all the paperwork signed, they were now legal partners. Joe left them and went home, while the other partners visited Silas's for a drink.

"To think this is where it all began months ago. Thanks to Silas," said Dan.

"No," said Mick. "It began with Sarah wanting a lift!"

10

Tom was very frustrated; over two weeks confined to the cottage. His feet were healing nicely all due to his wife's ministrations, and Sarah had gone shopping. 'Right,' thought Tom, 'opportunity knocks.' He carefully put on his thick socks. Then, very gingerly, he put his boots on. Tom stood up. It felt strange wearing boots again. His feet ached, but otherwise, he felt comfortable. He fancied a walk around the garden so off he went. He soon found what he was looking for - the little leather bag that he had carried for hundreds of miles. Sarah had placed the stinking morass (as she called it) inside an old stone jar, safe from rats, mice, and so on. Searching around the property, Tom found a few old plant pots, some cracked pottery - anything to hold compost. He carefully dug into the bottom of the compost heap, gathering enough for his needs. He filled every container he could find. He spread the contents of his small bag and delicately separated various pips and seeds and planted them into the pots. "Well, what are you up to?" Tom, so engrossed in his work, had not heard Sarah return. "Some of those pots can go on the window sills," she said, smiling. All the pots were put on the window sills. 'If it keeps Tom happy,' she thought, 'what does it matter if the cottage is upside down?'

Tom, by his labours, had developed a thirst. "I'm off to visit Silas," he said. "Pass the coat, please."

Sarah was horrified. "You cannot go out in that tatty old thing!"

Tom, for once, put his foot down and quietly said, "I will be wearing that coat." Sarah shrugged her shoulders. "Do as you damn well please." She realised that Tom did not have any money to purchase beer. "Here, take this," and she offered her husband a few coins.

"I do not need any money, thank you. There is plenty in this old coat."

Sarah scoffed; "Tom Pepper, I have washed that pile of rags three times. The lining has been removed to enable me and your daughter to make the repairs to it."

By this time, Tom had donned the old coat, fastened the buttons, and tied the belt. "Hold out your hands," he commanded his wife. Sarah scornfully did just that. Tom placed his right hand in the pocket of his coat. "Catch these," he said and placed two coins in Sarah's hand. Then he repeated it over and over. Sarah was shaking violently; never before had she held so much money in her hands. Tom stopped giving her any more coins. His wife, still shaking from shock, sat down. Tom, quite calmly, felt in his left-hand pocket. To Sarah's utter amazement, he held out a dirty, grubby clay pipe. She was well aware that Tom had the occasional smoke but smiled to herself as there was no baccy in the house. She could not believe what she was seeing. Tom had placed the pipe into his mouth and after a few puffs, it started to emit smoke! For some time, Sarah was in shock, then she slowly recovered. Standing up, she told Tom to raise his arms aloft. She felt into the pockets of the coat, and, to her satisfaction, found nothing!

"Open your hands, Tom Pepper. It is a wonderful illusion you have played on me." However, Tom's hands were as empty as his pockets. Sarah said, "Now reach into that damn coat and bring forth money." To her amazement, he did just that! The coins felt real, and the pipe was still warm. "Why can't I do that?" she asked.

"Because you do not have ultimate faith!" Tom ambled away towards the inn. "Just chewing the cud with Silas is what I need to do."

Sarah sat by the fire. She could not understand Tom's statement. "Not enough faith?" Sarah nearly exploded. "At least I go to church twice a week, far more than you do, Mr Pepper!"

As Tom entered the inn, he was aware that very little had changed since Martha had passed away. In the tap room, there were just a few regular drinkers about. "Tom Pepper!" exclaimed Silas. "Wonderful to see you!" Tom ordered his drink and put his hand in the coat, producing money to pay for the beer. "No, no," Silas thundered. "No Pepper will have to pay for his drink again as long as I run this inn!" Tom smiled; he had been half-expecting this response.

"Silas, just this once, allow me to pay, please." Silas reluctantly agreed. It was only then that he was aware of the coat Tom was wearing. For a few seconds he could not speak. As with Dennis long ago, he held out his hand. Tom placed two coins in his palm. Silas shook his head almost automatically, and this carried on until the beer was paid for.

"How did you acquire the coat?" asked Silas.

"I believe, according to Sarah and Don, that an old man left it." They had both described Dennis perfectly.

"I recall this very coat when Dennis wore it. How long ago was it? That is, when Dennis left the coat?"

Tom replied, "From what I can gather, it must be no longer than six months ago." Silas went pale and his hands were shaking.

"That cannot be right; Dennis passed away in his sleep well over a year ago!" Neither of them could work it out; both were convinced they were correct. Tom took a drink from Silas and went to the far end of the room, close to the fire. Unconsciously, Tom took the old pipe from his left-hand pocket, placed it in his mouth and started puffing. Slowly but surely, smoke began to rise from the pipe. Silas could not believe his eyes; it was as if Dennis was back. Completely and utterly dumbfounded and almost in a trance, he took Tom another pint. As he put the beer down on the table, he noticed something - there was no tobacco in the pipe!

'What a strange night,' Tom mused as he walked home. Such conflicting opinions concerning Dennis. Both could not be right, could they? Something niggled Tom; it was something Sarah had said about Dennis... then it clicked! Tom entered his home and a wonderful aroma drifted his way - fresh baked bread; lovely. He sat by the fire, got the toasting fork and toasted the bread over the fire. He had not had toast for a long time.

After consuming his meal, and with both of them now sitting by the fire, he began talking to Sarah. "One day, I am going to write a book about my travels," said Tom.

"You are going to write a book!? You cannot even write a letter!"

"True, but if I had some help, like from you for instance, I could dictate and you could jot it all down." What a wonderful idea! Now she would really know what had happened on Tom's travels. Up to now, he had seemed loath to talk about his trip.

Sarah then announced, "First thing in the morning, I will go to Carnforth. I can travel on Sam's bus." (Carnforth was a large town about ten miles away, and the buses only ran twice a week.)

Sarah left the next day as planned, taking money found in the old coat. Pens, pencils and writing pads were on her shopping list. What an ideal way of passing the long winter nights that lay ahead, and getting Tom to open up, but more importantly, to record his adventures.

Tom pottered about in the garden, not up to doing a full day's work yet. He was regaining his strength day by day. Don came out to exchange views on various matters concerning the fields, future crops and so on. At the finish of this planning session, Tom raised the subject of Dennis's visit. "When the old man came some months ago, what was you doing, Don?"

"Working in the bottom field, pruning hedges, weeding crops. It was the first chance I had since the heavy rains had finally stopped."

"What did you and the old man talk about?" Tom queried.

"Dennis told me to leave the top half of the field fallow, turn it over, and keep it weed-free. He said this was ideal soil for what is coming." "So, Dennis handled the soil; did he walk in the soil?" asked Tom.

"He did," replied Don. Tom had his answer; Sarah had told him that when Dennis took off his coat, he was dressed like a dandy! Only two pieces of the jigsaw to fit, so another talk with Silas and Sarah should complete the puzzle.

Throughout the long winter nights, very little was done, other than the laborious task of writing Tom's journal. Many a laugh, tears, frowns and doubts were expressed by Sarah. She could not understand or believe what Tom had said, but, true to her word, everything that Tom said was written down. Finally, the book was complete. Tom even signed his

name to signify that it was his tale. Very strangely, on the final blank page, he had put 'Post Script' then left it blank. Sarah questioned this. Tom replied, "That is for you to fill in."
"When do I fill the final page in?"

"Not till..." Tom would not discuss the matter further; instead, he began to talk about Dennis. "When Dennis visited, you gave him a cup of tea and a piece of cake. Tell me, did he drink the tea or eat the cake?"

Sarah thought about it, despite it being a strange question. "Now you mention it, I could have sworn he drank the tea and yet, when he had gone, I noticed the cup was still full. The cake, I found it on the floor untouched!"

The final part of the jigsaw had been fitted, Tom realised, but he said nothing.

During the visit he had paid Silas, amongst the many things they spoke about was the memory of Dennis. Silas began, "Dennis was not the tramp that he made himself out to be. About five miles from here is where Dennis lived. In fact, he owned a fair bit of land. All he ever grew were fruit crops - apples, pears, plums, etc. The year he passed away, late spring of that year, all the trees were full of blossom. For some unknown reason, two days or so after his death, every blossom fell to the earth. The trees rapidly rotted and the local farmers insisted they be pulled down and burned immediately." Tom shivered. His thoughts had been confirmed.

11

The years rolled by, and Don was courting a girl from the next village. Tom's fruit trees were doing fantastically well, and all the local gardeners and the like wanted cuttings. However, Tom always gave the same answer - "No, you can have some of the fruit at a small cost, but no cuttings." Some tried growing the seeds of the fruit, but all failed!

Tom was somewhat satisfied, the puzzle now complete. He recalled the last night with the old lady. He had difficulty understanding her strange words. As she handed him the bag of ripening fruit, she had said, very firmly, "For as long as the bearer of this fruit lives, the trees will blossom and their wares they will gift. When the bearer dies, no more gifts will flow. All parts of this gift will cease to grow." Her last words to him were even more strange - "I will visit you one day, but you will never know; others may see my presence!"

The years rolled on. In 1939, some fool in a far-off land was intent on causing trouble. Then came that fateful Sunday morning. Sarah and Tom caught the latter end of the Prime Minister's speech. "I have to say to you now, no such undertaking has been delivered. This nation is, therefore, at war with Germany!"

Tom grimaced, then turned the wireless off. "Not again," he groaned. Tom had seen the horrors of the First World War, so he was very sad. Sarah spoke not a word. She just clutched her husband's hands. "Don will want to fight for his country, just as I did. I dread the consequences," said Tom. Don joined the army in 1939, and he was not to see home again for over six years.

Sarah had moved to London to work for a high fashion chain, but 1941 saw her join the ATS. Food rationing came to the village in early 1940. It raised something of a smile, as with all the farms dotted about and some of the ladies working on the farm, few were very short of food. Other basics that were on ration and not available otherwise, these were missed. Whilst beer was never on ration, a great shortage of labour and raw materials meant that hotels, pubs, and inns. only received about a quarter of their usual needs. Most inns only opened for a short while each evening. The landlords imposed their own form of rationing!

Tom's orchards did not need a lot of attention so he had spare time on his hands. He was generally helping Jackson and Straw-man on their farms. Their sons had either joined up or been conscripted for the war effort. There were exemptions, of course; landowners and farmers could officially retain about 33% of their regular workforce, but other help had to be found ad-hoc!

12

The first few years of the war seemed to pass over the village, with very little disruption at all other than the rationing. However, 1943 saw a major change. A prisoner of war camp was hastily erected that year. The camp was around ten miles away, but some people got very concerned. They need not have worried. These were Italians, captured during the Desert War. Captured was perhaps too strong a word - most of them gave themselves up! It was a known fact that 4,000 of them surrendered to one British soldier! The soldier in question had got lost in the desert, and lacking water and food, he surrendered to the Italians. They were having none of it! After feeding and watering him, they lined up and told him, "We are prisoners of war; take us to your camp!" They pointed out the way and off they marched.

Most of them were sick and tired of the war, wanting nothing more than peace and quiet. So, they arrived at the camp. Guarded very strictly at first, it was soon apparent that none of them wanted to escape! Later that year, Italy broke from Germany and joined the Allies in fighting the Nazis. So, technically speaking, the men in the prison camp could not be regarded as enemies; neither could they be sent home to do the fierce fighting that was taking place. Restrictions were eased somewhat. Before, when they had worked on various farms, it would have been under armed escort. Now, as long as they obeyed the curfew rules, they could more or less do as they pleased, that is, work for whoever they wished! Some farms had a reputation of feeding them well. Others had land girls, or farmers' wives which was a big attraction to any young soldier. Two even worked at the Seven Bells pub doing various types of work. The landlady was seen to be a very generous person, giving free private lessons on various English ways! "And not all about learning the English language!" one local declared. He was immediately and indefinitely barred! Nothing much of note happened during the next two years, just a dramatic rise in the birth rate!

On May 8th 1945, victory was declared in Europe. Most were looking forward to the menfolk coming home. A few ladies in the village did not share their enthusiasm, as some were rather apprehensive.

Don did not return till the spring of the following year - "A little cleaning up had to be done," he informed his parents. The letter itself did not arrive until some weeks after the conclusion of hostilities. Tom and Sarah sat grim-faced in the kitchen. Don's "cleaning up" was no doubt due to the rumours they had heard and read, first on the radio, then through reports in the newspapers.

When Don finally came home, he looked very gaunt and worn out. He greeted his parents with a smile and a hug. Tom and Sarah were in tears, tears of joy! Their boy was home! Two days later, Don visited Silas. Silas said not a word for some time; they just hugged each other. Susan, Don's girlfriend, was also there. She had been helping Silas in various ways as Tom was too ill to come any more.

Don and Susan announced their wedding plans for that autumn. As a wedding present, Silas gave them the whole of the top floor of the inn. He would put a single bed in the parlour. He assured them it was getting more and more difficult to climb the stairs, however, the real reason of course was that they needed their privacy and also that he wanted them there! Don and his wife-to-be set about the upper floor. Walls and paintwork were stripped, and furniture and carpets given to the needy. The next few months flew by, and the upper floor looked magnificent. Don and Susan were very pleased with their endeavours.

Tom and Sarah had visited the local doctors regarding Tom's illness. Their last visit had left them both stunned. "I can do no more for you, Mr Pepper; your illness is terminal. At best, you have two, maybe three years to live. You will, over that period, get weaker and weaker, and, in the final months, I am afraid you will be bedridden. I will, of course, upgrade the strength of your medication when required."

By the time of Don's wedding, Tom felt well enough to attend. "No alcohol!" his doctor had stated. Don had taken over the licence of the inn and to Silas's chagrin, started selling food - crisps, cheese snacks, nuts and raisins. "This inn is not a café!" Silas had stated. "It's a pub, i.e., beer, wines, spirits. Not food!"

Don just grinned. "Have to move with the times!"

"And another thing, why have you changed the name of the inn?" Don and Susan had renamed the inn "Mimms Inn".

A few months later, Susan announced that she was expecting. "Whatever you do," Silas said on hearing the news, "please promise you will not name the child after me if it is a boy!" Both vowed that the child would not be named Silas.

The christening of the child was held the following year. The vicar stated, "I name this child Thomas Aliss Pepper." Tom and Sarah were very happy, as was Silas. 'They kept their word,' he thought and, of course, he was right... was he not?

13

Sarah's wedding to Garth, her fiancé, was looming fast. "No, no, no. I will not be married in some posh church in London. I will be wed at the church in the village where I was born or not wed at all!" Thus, Sarah stated her intentions to her prospective in-laws.

Garth's mother spoke up, "But the guest list alone is over the 400 mark; your church could not hold them!"

"Then keep the guest list to less than 40!" snarled Sarah.

"Not possible," answered the mother. "Who could we leave out?"

"Leave them all out, otherwise the wedding is off!" Sarah removed her glove, took off the very expensive engagement ring, put it on the table and walked away.

Garth's father had not said a word during the wedding plans but he was thoroughly enjoying it. 'Some woman; some lady! My son has chosen well - put that old cow back in her place. And if my son is half the man I believe he is, he will certainly chase after this wonderful creature!' All these were private thoughts by Garth's father, not to be spoken aloud!

The wedding took place at the village church in the late autumn of that year. Tom held his daughter's hand as they walked down the aisle. Close behind, Don was pushing the wheelchair, but Tom had insisted that he could manage the few steps it would take to reach the vicar. The church was full. Of the forty guests invited from Garth's side of the family, only twenty-three managed the journey. Reasons for not coming were numerous - other commitments, falling ill, etc. Tom and Sarah invited no one; there was no need! Rule of thumb was if you feel like coming, you are most welcome! The reception, of course, was held at the inn. A lovely little spread; most enjoyable. Meal finished, tables and chairs were stacked against the walls and dancing took place. Garth's parents danced alongside the other guests, then a sing-song took place at which most sang. Late in the evening, Sarah and her husband left for their honeymoon - a month in St Tropez! Tom was absolutely worn out, so Don insisted on pushing his father home, which pleased his mum.

Sarah and Garth were having a great time on honeymoon; they only had a few days left then back home to London. Suddenly, the hotel manager came to them on the beach. "An urgent phone call," he said. A private plane was arranged, and the nearest railway to the airport was sourced, then their final few miles were by taxi. Unfortunately, the road was blocked as fallen trees and other debris barred the way. "Right, Shanks's pony is called for!" announced Sarah. Garth did not understand; there were no ponies out here! After walking for a short while, Sarah recognised the area. They were only a short walk from Straw-man's farm. In the semi-darkness, they entered the farmyard.

"Are we required to walk through that?" Garth pointed to various heaps of animal droppings.

"Don't be so toffee-nosed! Cow shit is all that is," Sarah rebuked him.

Straw-man came out to greet them, listened to their concerns and then spoke. "No use lending thee 'oss and coach if all roads are blocked. Can thy man ride an 'oss?"

Sarah smiled. "Can Garth ride a horse? Why, he has just missed out on a place in the equestrian events at the forthcoming Olympics!" Two of Straw-mans' best hunters were saddled. Sarah and Garth mounted. "Quickest way is over yon fields," explained Straw-man, but before he could open the gate, his horses ran past him and both jumped over the gate!

Sarah jumped off the horse and flew up the path. Garth, as any rider should do, was to take care of the horses. He searched around various sheds and found the tack that Silas had given Don many years ago. Along with some rags, he began grooming the horses. 'Magnificent horseflesh; rarely have I seen better. I must introduce myself to Mr Straw. I have money to invest, and he, in turn, has land that can be used. I am beginning to like this man. I could, I suppose, buy property nearby, or even have a house built for me. I like these people, for when help is needed, it is swiftly given, unlike London.' All these thoughts and more flashed through his mind as he groomed the horses. He found some hay and duly fed them. Taking a clean bucket, he walked down to the little stream nearby. It took three journeys to quench the horses' thirst. This done, he tied the horses to a fence, put the lovely saddles in one of the sheds for safety, and, with a heavy heart, made his way to the cottage. As he entered, it struck him that not a word was being spoken. Tom's wife and two children were sat around the bed.

The doctor had called late in the evening. "Just a matter of hours now; he will feel no further pain," he had said. Sarah was aware of the good doctor's reputation in that he had helped many, ensuring their final hours were as comfortable as possible. The good doctor would have been horrified to know that it was common knowledge that he had gone far beyond what was acceptable in his profession, and that he had helped so many over the "last hurdle", so to speak. Sarah was very grateful to the kindly old man.

Two hours ticked by, then suddenly, Tom rose up. "No evidence, no evidence..." Tom's eyes were not focused on anything; he was just wild-eyed. They helped him to lie down, but no one could tell if he was gurgling for breath or trying to laugh! A few moments later, he passed away.

Sarah sat by his side till daybreak, holding his now-cold hands. 'Someone has to be strong,' she thought.

Don and his sister were given instructions - Don was to fetch Ted, while Sarah was to call for the vicar. Garth just wandered away to take care of the horses and other stock. "Mum, Mum, it's snowing!" her daughter shouted. "Not snow; blossom from the fruit trees!"

Ted and Vicar Drabble arrived around midday, one to take Tom away and prepare him for his funeral. The vicar was told in no uncertain terms, "No long-winded sermon; the full service must take no more than one half-hour. Two hymns will be sung; number 1 - All Things Bright and Beautiful, and number 2 - To Be a Pilgrim; that is all," insisted Sarah. The date of the funeral was to be in five days' time. Vicar Drabble pointed out that John Bunyan's works were seldom allowed in the Church of England, so he would prefer it if she would choose another hymn.

"You believe in speaking openly and honestly, do you not, vicar?"

"Of course, it is the only way to live."

"Then you will not mind me asking your wife a question then?"

"I do not mind at all," replied the vicar. "May I enquire what question you are going to ask my wife?"

"Of course I will tell you. Myself and a few of the regular congregation are puzzled, because when you go on your annual seminars, a certain lady always goes on holiday at the same time." Amazingly, Sarah got her way; Pilgrim's Progress was allowed at Tom's funeral.

14

No fire was lit that day. No food was consumed; the table was bare. Sarah sighed for the first time since she and Tom had moved in all those years ago. She gave one final sigh and then prepared herself for the day's events. Not many mourners were expected - Silas was suffering from a chest infection, and Jackson's legs now refused to work as instructed. 'Yes,' she thought, 'the grim reaper will no doubt be paying many visits in the near future.'

The hearse arrived on time, but there were no other cars. Sarah had told Ted, "I am in no hurry to say goodbye to Tom, so myself and my children will walk behind." As they started on this sad journey, Sarah was a little surprised. It was a village custom that when a funeral was taking place, people would gather at their gates to show respectfulness, but none did so.

Silas had made it almost halfway up the hill. He dearly wanted to attend Tom's interment but he could not walk another step. "Nah then, lad, tha looks in a wos state than me." Jackson, with the aid of his sons, managed to rise from the wheelchair. "Sit thee sen down, Silas; two of me lads can drag me up yon hill." The hearse travelled slowly up the hill towards the church.

Sarah, her arm linked to her son's, was very weary. Lack of sleep and food were taking their toll. Don sensed this and helped her the best he could. "We should have hired a car, but no, Mother insisted we walk," Sarah whispered to Don.

"At least it will be a small funeral, then home for a long rest." However, Don knew different. He was now the landlord of the inn. Over the last few days, he had heard rumours about who was going to be at the funeral, etc. That his father was well-liked was obvious. They turned the last corner; just a few more steps to the church. Don, his sister Sarah, Garth and Don's mother were totally amazed. On the pavement outside the church stood a large crowd. Men were doffing their hats, ladies' heads were bowed, and there were flowers everywhere. Just beyond the church, a Rolls Royce was parked.

Except for Don, they were all overwhelmed as they had never seen a bigger turnout for one person. Just beyond the Rolls Royce stood a beautiful black carriage. In the shafts were black horses, their brasses gleaming. John Straw had come then. "Why do these good people not wait in church? For the older ones, it is quite cool today."

"Because the church is full," Don answered. They made their way up the church path. Don was aware that his mother was on the point of collapse, so he gripped her tightly. Entering the church, Sarah understood her son. The church was packed; not even any standing-room. Straw-man and his family, Jackson, Jane and their sons, Joe Platts... all were there. Sarah then spotted Silas, trying to rise from the wheelchair! 'Silas in a wheelchair, the wonderful old fool,' Sarah thought.

The sermon went quite smoothly, for a start anyway. During the ramblings of Vicar Drabble, Sarah's eyes wandered to the far end of the church. A lovely stained-glass window? She shook her head. 'Tiredness and hallucinations,' Sarah thought. She had a fleeting vision of an old lady giving a Mona Lisa-type smile but Sarah never spoke of her alleged vision - people would say she was cracking up!

The first hymn had been sung, and now it was time for the last one. "Unfortunately, the organist cannot find the music for the final hymn. I have chosen a replacement." The old vicar prayed that the Almighty would take him at that very instant or that he would have to resign immediately this service was over. He really loved this old church; it had served many of the surrounding villages for centuries. The organist had sprung the news that she would not play the chosen hymn just as the congregation were entering the church. Looking around the bemused people, some wept openly. Somehow, he would have to finish the service.

The organist asked the verger to work the wind pumps for the organ, as she was going to play her choice of music! The verger stood up but never said a word; just spat in her face! "Quiet, please," remarked Garth's father, Sir John, in a calm but strong voice. "With the good vicar's permission, I have a few words to say." Meanwhile, Lady Pru, his wife, was having a quiet word with Don. At the end of their conversation, both nodded in agreement. Lady Pru then approached the vicar. "Tell that evil creature to vacate the organ seat immediately!" The vicar told the organist to leave, but she refused to obey! Without another word, Lady Pru took off her coat, and approached the organ, talons poised! The organist gazed in horror at this hideous woman who was advancing towards her. Coat thrown on the floor, her features were set in pure evil, and her long fingernails painted red. The organist fled the church never to enter it again. The verger, leaning on the organ, was howling with laughter. Lady Pru approached him as if to console him, but a swift knee to the nether regions soon quietened him! "Start to pump the bellows when I tell you to, alright?" The verger just nodded, riddled with pain and laughter. He thought to himself, 'The wife is going to get plenty of rest over the next few nights!'

Sir John stood in front of the congregation. "With the family's kind permission, I will give a eulogy on the life of Tom Pepper. I only met Tom twice, but I realised even then what a good man he was. Until today, I never imagined how greatly he was loved by so many. For a man to venture on the journey that he took was amazing. No plans, no knowledge of his destination, no backup… some achievement. The finest thing Tom ever did was when he gave his assent that my oaf of a son could marry his wonderful daughter."

Lady Pru piped up, "Regarding your oaf of a son, blood will tell!"

Sir John doffed his imaginary hat and bowed to the lady. "If I may continue, one thing Tom and I share is that both of us have such wonderful wives. I met my wife-to-be many, many years ago. It took her at least six months to ask me for a date. (Lady Pru sniffed.) It took a further nine months for her to propose marriage!"

"If it had been left to you, I would still be a spinster!" she yelled.

"May I continue? The point I am getting to is that Tom had something I lacked - courage; sheer raw courage. How he made his journey, how he stumbled the last few miles home, none of us will ever know. To repeat, Tom had a wonderful wife who guided him when needed, and let him live his dream. For myself, I treasure the minute, hour, day, and year when my adorable wife proposed. To me, I lacked what Tom had plenty of - guts! Now, to the last hymn, Tom's choice. A very apt one - 'To Be a Pilgrim'. The battle-axe will play the organ and I will sing. Please, please, join in."

In a wonderful tenor voice, he began. Sir John had sung a few notes when an equally wonderful voice joined in - the deep baritone of the vicar! The old church had never witnessed the like. A knight and a vicar, hand in hand, singing at the top of their voices, their free hand extolling all to join in, and they did, including those outside. The final line of the first verse - 'His first avowed intent, to be a pilgrim' - really summed Tom's life up. Tom was laid to rest facing the hills and valleys he loved, then they gathered outside the church to exchange farewells.

Suddenly, Silas spoke up. "A funeral tea is being held at the inn, including free drinks." He then glared at the packed crowd; "And should anyone offer to pay, they will be barred for life!" Don had not the heart to tell Silas he was in no position to bar anyone! Don held the licence, not Silas! Sarah just wanted to go home; she was worn out, but good manners dictated that she should attend the tea. However, after about an hour, she made her excuses and left with her daughter and son-in-law. "Shall I go ahead and light the fire and put the kettle on, Mum?" asked young Sarah.

"There is no need. The fire will be ablaze, the kettle gently steaming and a vase of flowers on the table, and maybe, just maybe, a letter there."

"But we left an empty house this morning; are you dreaming, Mother?"

Sarah gave a wan smile, then said, "Your father told me this would occur."

Sarah sat by the fire, which had been lit as she had said. Her daughter made cups of tea, still shaking her head in bewilderment. How did her mother know? Sitting by the fire, Sarah's mind travelled back over the day's events. The conflict of emotions was tremendous. First, the sadness at taking Tom to his resting place, then her exhaustion after climbing that hill, the expectancy of a small funeral, and on arrival, her total amazement that so many had come to pay their respects to Tom. Then there was the sorrow of entering the church, the anger and frustration of the cancelling of Tom's favourite hymn, the venom and determination shown first by the verger, and then Lady Pru, and after that, screams of panic and fright from the organist in fear of her life! The sad old vicar was no doubt praying that he would be swallowed up. There was the repartee between the knight and his lady (it must have taken many years of practice to reach that level). The eulogy by Sir John had been just perfect. The knight and the vicar, hand in hand - amazing singing by all. Sarah lay back in the chair and threw the unopened letter onto the fire. Her last thoughts as she dozed off were of Tom, lying in his coffin wearing only 'The Old Tramps Coat'.

Copy of Tom's last letter entitled

"Not Till"

I will wait for thee
By the garden gate.
It matters not
If thou art late,
For there we will plan
And travel afar
To discover what lays
Beyond the far-most star!

Milton Keynes UK
Ingram Content Group UK Ltd.
UKHW042238040124
435471UK00006B/240

9 781805 414988